When She Sleeps

Leora Krygier

when she sleeps

The Toby Press

First Edition 2004

The Toby Press LLC

POB 8531, New Milford, CT. 06676-8531, USA
& POB 2455, London WIA 5WY, England
www.tobypress.com

ISBN 1 59264 086 9 *hardcover* original

A CIP catalogue record for this title is
available from the British Library

Typeset in Garamond by Jerusalem Typesetting

Printed and bound in the United States
by Thomson-Shore Inc., Michigan

for David

And Pharaoh spoke unto Joseph; in my dream,
Behold I stood upon the brink of the river.

Genesis 41:17

Mai

The night we returned to Saigon, my mother, Linh, exacted the last promise I would ever make to her, my vow never to call her "Mother" again. We'd just arrived in the city before dusk, Grandmother Thanh, Linh and I, hiding until twilight sank the last of the hot sun, then we emerged with the others, all the ghosts from the countryside. Like them, we were homeless, carrying our kerosene stoves and torn mats on our backs, shadows looking for work and shelter in the city. We found a space on the bottom landing of a cracked stairwell, and made our beds there, on the concrete, still splintered with old shrapnel. I was almost asleep when Linh whispered to me and made me the accomplice in her crime.

"Every name is its own world, every word a journey," Linh began. "Promise me, Mai, swear it," she said, taking hold of my hands. "Give me your word you won't call me mother, only Linh from now on."

I waited for my eyes to adjust to the dark and looked at her closely. Before the takeover, she'd been a lecturer in linguistics at the University of Saigon. She was a teacher of etymology, skilled at exhuming the origins of words, finding their buried secrets; for her a name was an entire history, a universe, not to be disturbed, never to be erased or forgotten.

I hesitated to answer, but she pressed me.

"Mai, please."

"I promise."

It was then I made my own oath—I would let her rob me of this intimacy, but I'd never let her take anything else from me again.

"Say it now," she demanded, emboldened. "Say my name."

"Yes, Linh," I said, watching her, then looking away.

She was reckless with her own promises, a charlatan. She was stealing the word from me, doing exactly what she professed to despise, making "Mother" extinct, lost to me, but I knew I couldn't do otherwise. I'd seen her eyes find a fleck of light in the black coal of the stairwell when I said her name. I knew Saigon was the place of her fall, her surrender, and now that we'd returned, she needed to have her name said aloud, and repeated. I understood then that every time her name was uttered, it gave her strength, and reminded her that her spirit existed.

"It's not called Saigon anymore. They renamed it Ho Chi Minh City," Linh said, without sadness.

I was exhausted from our three-day walk back to the city and I didn't care that Boulevard Charner was now Nguyen Hue, or Rue Catinat was Dong Khoi. Only Linh cared about the exchanging of names, the substitution of words, one for another. For me, they were a waste of breath, here, in a place where words did not matter. She blamed others for taking away the names—but she was the one who was a thief.

Linh was worse now, two years after the tanks had crashed through the presidential palace. Her madness came and went more often. She was a wick, sometimes burnt out; at other times, a flame. Often, she didn't know where she was, who she was, but she taught me French during the day and English at night. She closed her eyes and repeated the sounds softly, like lullabies, told me the names of things, made me pronounce them over and over.

"Say it again, Mai. Don't forget."

"Yes, Linh," I said, and I was now a foot soldier in the war of words she waged against herself.

I took to English faster than French. Maybe it was because she taught me English in the soft of night, as we lay down together in the dark, the gloominess our blanket against the daylight. And English became my language of darkness, my language of sleep.

"Repeat it, Mai," Linh said, and I liked that my name sounded like the English "my," that it meant a belonging to something, someone. Then Linh told me there were no belongings, only longings. "Now that you're thirteen, you're almost a woman, and you need to know."

Even that Linh tried to take away from me, even my belonging.

When the first heat of dawn crept onto our backs, we packed up our mats and disappeared into the mist of a new daybreak. I didn't remember much about the city I was born in, and there was nothing I liked about it that morning. It was dirty, bunker-gray, with gutters of refuse. A wave of bicycles and cyclos filled the streets with their sharpened edges.

The cyclos never came near my grandmother.

Even they knew to stay away from Thanh.

"Where are we going?" I asked Thanh.

Thanh replied we couldn't go back to the villa. Someone else was living in it now, and it would never belong to us again.

Maybe Linh was right—maybe there was no belonging, only longing.

After a week in the city, Thanh found our cousin, Van, selling rice pancakes on a street near the Rex Hotel. At first, Van didn't recognize Thanh. In the two years we had been away from the city, her hair had turned bright white, angry as the lightning bolts that punched open the night skies. But when she called out his name, he remembered the rattle in her voice and we went to live with him, his new wife, Luong, and their girl. Van had been married before, but his first wife and child had been killed in the war.

I didn't understand how he'd forgotten his first born, as if another child could replace the one that was taken from him.

Thanh made the arrangements. Linh would help Van sell his pancakes on the street and we would come to live with them in their room. It was one of Thanh's barters, her clever trades, as if my mother, beautiful Linh, was something that could be bought and sold on the black market.

Luong had a small face and a burn across her chest from the war that seared deeper than her skin. She was not happy to share the small room with three more. The room was empty of furniture, but it was better than the thatched houses and dried-mud walls we'd been living in. There, far from the main roads, we'd slept on dirty, straw mats, the lice finding their way into Linh's thick, raven hair.

Ho Chi Minh City was ugly—but the Rex Hotel was still there, just like Linh had described to me on our way back to Saigon, a crown perched on top of its sixth story. I stole into the hotel every opportunity I had, and hid behind the palm trees and flowers, the cages of singing birds. I looked up at the ceiling fans, watched them go round, cut the thick air with their paddles. There were no Americans in Ho Chi Minh City now, only Russians, and I watched them—fat tourists sitting in rattan chairs, drinking iced coffee, until someone chased me away. I sneaked into many places, but I always came back to the Rex. When Thanh couldn't find me, she knew I'd be there, looking for him, Linh's American, my father. I knew his name. I'd even remembered seeing him a few times, as if in a dream, when I was small, but I called him only Linh's American, because his name had no place here with us in this broken city.

I knew he'd come back to the Rex, not the Majestic or the Caravelle, not the Continental Hotel. He'd come to the Rex because that's where he often met Linh. They'd meet before five o'clock, when the briefing room was crowded with rows of chairs and an officer announced the day's sorties. She would walk right in front of the podium, just before they listed the contacts with the enemy. She told me she'd do it on purpose, as a kind of mark, an emphasis, the way she used to underline the paragraphs in her university notebooks.

Don't forget where you are.

This is not your country.

Twenty-nine contacts with the enemy, the briefing officer had announced that afternoon.

"E-ne-my," Linh repeated to me, a week after we came to live in Van's apartment. "When the enemy comes, even the women must fight. These are the things you must remember. Don't forget, Mai, enemy, Scotch and water, North and South."

Linh's American drank Scotch and water.

She didn't have to repeat it to me. I understood how the sounds were strung together, like beads on a necklace. They weren't strange, foreign, to me. After all, it was his tongue. English was the language of my father.

"North and South. It has always been a struggle between the two, Mai," she explained. "Vietnam was born of a fight between two dragons. So intent were they to obtain a sacred pearl, their intertwined bodies fell into the China Sea to form the land."

Her words conjured the image in my mind, and I saw the bodies of the dragons, how they twisted like snakes around the water. This was Linh's power over me, the way she called up words to do her bidding.

The next day, I followed a chambermaid and slipped into one of the Rex's vacant rooms. Inside, I opened the closet door, pulled out all the drawers, looked under the bed. I didn't expect to find anything, but I was a scout, sniffing and scratching at what was left behind, the traces. I turned on every light, and ran the water in the bathtub and the sink at the same time, heard it rush over the porcelain. Afterward, I sat down on a chair, surveyed the bed that stood like a throne, a temple in the middle of the room. It called out to me, daring me, and I stared at it, craving it.

Then I pulled back the sheets; they were white and cool, ironed. The pillows were soft, with a scent of lemon peel. It was the rainy season, and the rain pounded the roof, falling in torrents outside the window. The streets were rivers of water, but I was in a big bed, in its ocean of linens. I fell asleep dreaming under the hum of the ceiling fan.

I woke up with a heat between my legs.

※

It is Linh's heat.

After the briefing, Linh and the American go up to the roof of

*the Rex and order drinks. They watch the day bleed slowly into night,
see the night consume the city, ravage her once again. The roof sags with
the weight of khaki, correspondent suits and uniforms, and the city dims
into blindness below them.*

It is there he tells her.

He is going back.

She knows.

*She's heard him say that before. He is always leaving, going away
and coming back and he seems to exist only in his comings and goings.*

*They return to his hotel room and she looks around. His room is
neat, orderly; books piled one on top of the other, like columns of words
in a dictionary. It is a neatness that cries out, blocks out the rumbling
in the hallways, in the streets, the skies of flares.*

*Linh makes love with her American and she feels the heat of
his breath on her neck, a fire, and suddenly there is no air in the hotel
room, no more breath, because he takes up all of Linh, and he is taking
it away with him.*

He is going away.

*She sits up on the bed and cries, the tears staining the whiteness
of the sheets. He says he will find a way to be with her, he promises, to
be with her and the baby that rises in her belly like a mountain. He
kisses her again and she holds him, then pushes him away and brings
him close.*

*She can also come and go, ebb away and flow back to him, like
the coastline against the China Sea, the back of the dragon.*

Go.

*It is the monsoon season, and it is pouring. Linh starts to talk, but
the rain outside thunders in her head and she knows she isn't making
sense. The words are always so pretty, colored plumes, baskets of fruits in
the market, spilling over, the tiniest of treasures. She collects the words,
every one, a nuance, a subtly of meaning, and they are her salvation,
her sanity, but they rebel against her now. Like watercolors in the rain,
her words run together, fall into each other. She is speaking English and
Vietnamese and French all at once, and he doesn't understand what she
is saying.*

The language is fading away from her. It gathers up like clouds at sunset, then dissipates in a moment. If only she could be clearer, more precise. If only she could find the right phrase, turn it around, inside out, maybe he would understand her.

   Maybe, he wouldn't leave her.

Mai

Grandmother Thanh boiled the rice in the tiny kitchen of Van's apartment, her hands commanding the weak fire not to sputter out. For a moment, she almost looked content, as though the darkened pots were one of her precious adding machines, the ones she'd mastered once, when Grandfather had been alive and owned a silk business.

"Why doesn't Linh know how to cook?" I asked her.

A month before, Linh attempted to do the evening cooking, burning the little rice we had, and from then on, it was Thanh who prepared the meal for the three of us every night.

Thanh was cutting the last of the cabbage and though she usually didn't like to answer my questions, something came over her when she stood over the stove. As the water bubbled, her tongue loosened along with a strand of hair from her tight bun and I sat like a cat, waiting for my chance to ask her my questions about Linh.

I want to know.

Tell me about her.

"Your Grandfather spoiled Linh," Thanh finally answered, and there was a fierceness in the way she pronounced Linh's name, in the way she pushed her tongue into her upper teeth, like oil bubbling up from beneath the earth's surface. "We had a big house and a nanny, and a maid to do the cooking, with another girl to do the washing. Two house-boys and three maids," Thanh said, banging her words together.

Two plus three, I saw her calculating her losses in her mind. "Go on."

"Linh's father, your grandfather, was an important man, very rich," Thanh continued. "Linh learned French and English at the *lycée*. And when the Americans came, your grandfather worked with them too. Until he became sick and everything changed."

I watched Thanh at the stove and I wasn't sure I believed her about the villa and the servants. She seemed too practiced, at ease with our deprivation. She was too familiar with wheedling; too used to the taste of a poor man's tea, to have ever been a rich man's wife.

I looked outside the window. It was almost time for the evening meal and Linh would be home soon. I kept asking Thanh questions while she cooked and she started to tell me something about Linh, but then changed her mind. Instead, she told me again about the legend of Quan Am, the Goddess of Mother and Child.

"She was turned out of her house and spent her life begging on the streets."

It was Thanh's favorite story, and each time she repeated it, her sigh sunk her eyes deeper into their sockets, as if she were Quan Am herself, as though she wore Quan Am's yoke of suffering on her own shoulders.

"I do everything for you. The two of you would be dead by now without me."

"I want to hear about Linh."

"Stop pestering me, Mai."

With the way I looked, Thanh said I should be grateful she hadn't sent me away to the nuns, that she hadn't abandoned me, cast me out like Quan Am.

"You're *bui doi,* Mai."

It was the name they gave half-breeds like me. It meant "dust of the earth". She thought saying it would cut me like her cabbage knife, but it only strengthened my resolve. Even dust could be a weapon, blind a man.

I knew I had some of the features of Linh's American. I looked at myself in Thanh's little silver mirror, one of the few belongings she'd saved for herself from the old villa, and I saw that my nose came out too far from my face, my eyes were too round. I was already a head taller than graceful Linh, an awkward excess, which didn't seem to belong here.

"Do I look like him?" I asked.

"No," Thanh said. "He left you nothing."

Linh had promised he'd come back for us soon, but it was two years since the fall of Saigon, three years since I'd last seen him, just before the Americans pulled out their troops. But I didn't remember much about him. Thanh always made sure to keep me away whenever he'd come to see Linh. At first, I believed Linh. I was certain he'd come the month before the Northern army slithered down into the South. I remembered the curfew that closed down the city. Loudspeaker trucks had blared out, and there had been the sound of gunfire and explosions in the distance. In the streets, there were television sets, refrigerators people had tried to sell for cash. One by one, the beautiful villas on Pasteur Boulevard were boarded up and Thanh exchanged her last piasters for gold on the black market when South Vietnamese money became worthless.

But he didn't come for us.

"They never leave you anything but their pain. They sell it to you like sweet cakes, and you buy it, even though you know it's spoiled, a bad bargain," Thanh shook her head.

The week before the *Cong-san* captured the city, Thanh begged Linh to go to the consular offices to get exit visas. She'd heard they were giving out *laissez-passers* at the movie theater, but still Linh wouldn't budge, wouldn't leave her bed.

He'll come to get us, Linh had mumbled over and over again. He'd promised.

By then, even Thanh, who'd despised Linh's American, had begun to pray that he would return, and get us out of Saigon before it collapsed.

Still, he didn't come for us.

Then the guns were closer and smoke choked the air. Rockets landed, slamming into buildings. The last day, Linh finally agreed to go to the American embassy. We were in the crowd that pushed against the gates, trying to climb over the high walls of the compound. Linh held my hand tight. Thanh was sure we'd get in. After all, Linh had been there many times before.

She'd eaten cheeseburgers and French fries with him at the restaurant inside.

She'd sat by the pool, but Linh's American was gone now and no one recognized her.

Thanh yelled out to a Marine, but we couldn't make our way through.

I heard the wind of dust, the terrible noise from the helicopters landing on the roof pad and then the silence when they stopped coming. There was only the mewing of Radio Hanoi on a far off transistor.

People ran in every direction. Some burned South Vietnamese uniforms in the street and ashes from the fires floated everywhere. We followed the crowd to the harbor and saw the few ships that remained. We stood at the dock, but as much as Thanh tried to bully her way through to the front of the line, we couldn't get on a boat. Night fell and it turned dark. Except for the bullhorns and the sound of the soldiers yelling, the city was a tomb.

"Will Linh's American come back for us?" I asked Thanh.

"It doesn't matter now."

He didn't even come when we each packed one bag and left Saigon for the south. He didn't return when we walked for days, and slept by the side of the road, the night black as tar.

It was then that I began to realize I couldn't believe Linh anymore. Maybe she'd dreamed him up, made up all the stories she'd told me about her tall American.

"Will Linh get better?"

"It's the American, it's his fault," Thanh spat on the floor. "She hasn't been herself since she met him at that party. I don't understand my stubborn daughter. She wasn't one of those streetwalkers, the hookers from the Dragon Bar off Le Loi Boulevard who ran after the GI's."

Linh spoke flawless English and had been invited to tea at the British embassy. She'd attended dinners at the U.S. ambassador's villa as a guest of the German military attaché and had friends who were journalists at the *Saigon Daily News.* The best seamstresses in Saigon sewed her *ao dais,* tunics of the softest silk, slit long and effortless.

I shook my head.

Thanh didn't know her own daughter, but I did.

It wasn't her exquisite tunics that separated Linh from all the others—it was her language.

The words were Linh's silk. Thanh stopped cooking for a moment.

"We had a beautiful house with a garden of flowers, and a chauffeur to take Grandfather to work each day," she said, looking out from Van's dingy window to the street. "It's good your grandfather is dead. It's better he doesn't know what's happened to his wife and daughter, his little *con lai,* his half-breed granddaughter."

"But—"

"Enough," Thanh said. "Don't speak about this to anyone. No one must know who we once were.

"It's Linh who speaks without thinking and puts us in danger."

It was Linh we'd worried about, on the road, in the villages. It was Linh and her sudden outbursts that could have sent us all to the reeducation camps.

Linh and her words, not me.

The door opened, and Linh came in from her day of selling rice pancakes on the street. She looked exhausted and didn't even hang her straw *non* on the wall peg near the door. She let the hat fall to the floor and I saw the three lines that ran hard on her forehead like creeks.

Thanh waved me off to bring Linh a wet rag. Linh lay down on the floor and I washed off her hands, then her feet. Her small hands and feet were still callused from the time she'd been forced to work in the fields.

Linh sat up.

"Da Lat. We have to go to Da Lat," she suddenly announced. "He won't find us here. We have to go there now."

Fury rose in my throat. All the time we'd hidden in the back-country, Linh had begged to go back to Saigon. Even Thanh had become tired of her ranting and had finally relented. Now that we were in Saigon, Linh cried for Da Lat.

"He'll remember the old summer home," Linh persisted. "He'll look for us there. I promise you he'll be there," she pleaded.

"Stop it, Linh. I don't want to hear your lies," I yelled at her, and like paper, her shoulders crumpled into her chest. She stayed that way for a moment, but then her body found air somehow and she sat up once again and looked at me.

"You don't understand. It's a place of words, where they find a home. In Da Lat the trees and the water give them a seamless silhouette, a shadow, a thread that leads one to another. That's why we must go back there."

Her voice was vapor, dampening my fury, and my head became full with her bewitchment. I had to think hard and clear not let it happen again, not to lose myself in her madness, not to be dragged down and drown in her silt. And then I knew how he felt—how Linh's American had come under her spell, how she used her words as enchantments.

Thanh gave us each a bowl of rice.

"My Linh has lost her smile," Thanh said, and it was the first time my grandmother looked as though she felt sorry for Linh. Then she took on a look of bemusement. "Even a murderer keeps her smile."

"A murderer?"

"Never mind. Eat your food before Luong returns."

With all we'd lost, who cared if Linh had lost her smile? Besides, Linh did smile. I'd seen her smile when she slept. Every night, she prepared herself for sleep, as if she were packing to go on a long trip, looking forward to it. And when she fell asleep, Linh slept deeply. I'd seen her eyelids flutter, watched her lips open slightly as they softened into a smile. She must have been dreaming about other times. It was the only time she let me touch her—in her sleep, the only time she let me smooth down her beautiful, long hair.

I too wanted to dream of other times, but as much as I tried, I had none to recall. I had no memories of villas and gardens, trips to the zoo, the fresh linen on the beds, servants and amahs. They weren't my memories.

Then I recalled the dream I had at the Rex.

I wanted to feel it again, taste it, Linh and her American. I wanted to know him, learn all the things she hadn't told me about him, and become her, if only in the night.

So I did something I had no right to do, something I should have regretted, but I didn't. After Linh fell asleep, I slept beside her, and crept in as close as I could. Next to her, it was as if I'd slipped back inside her, returning to her womb.

I took them over then, her memories, unlocking them, and seizing them for myself. Thanh had once told me that a person could dream someone else's dreams, their recollections. Just like the blood that flowed between mother and daughter, even sisters, so too dreams could stream from one person to another, make a journey, she explained, like a basket down a river, for someone else to find. And that's what I did.

I was only following Linh's example, her thievery, and I too became a bandit, stealing her memories from her, dreaming her life. I should have asked myself what would become of her if I took all her memories from her, but I thought only of myself—that Linh had given me nothing and her dreams were mine to now take and give away.

※

It is in Ha Long Bay, among its limestone islands, where heaven and earth mixes, floats in a thick mist. It is there, long before the country is hacked in two, before it is a north and a south, severed. Linh has never seen the three thousand tiny islands that rise jagged from its clear, emerald waters, but her father has told her stories about the grottoes that appear, born of wind and waves. There are giant caves, gaping walls dripping with water, chambers of rocks. To the east are coral reefs, sleeping beneath the water's surface.

Linh likes to hear her father's stories about Ha Long, its legends and riddles. He is a quiet man, soft, like the clouds of Ha Long's sky. Linh likes him for his gentleness, like the gurgles of mothers to their babies, their half-words.

She doesn't understand his marriage to a woman like Thanh, a woman of coarse words, severed chords. Her speech is rough, gratings against rocks. Even the sips of viperine from the bottle she hides, its small snake still curled up on the bottom, do not soften the sounds that come from her throat.

Her father tells Linh that Ha Long means descent of the dragon. It is where a great dragon wakes from a deep sleep and descends into the sea, where he shakes his tail to part land and water to make thousands of islands like beads of jade.

Linh is invited to a party at the American embassy. She arrives by taxi. Stepping out of the car, she looks at the exterior of the compound. There is a spiked grille, floodlights, a tower with Marine guards on top. Inside, the room is all tiny Christmas lights. Everyone seems to be talking at once, and in the background there are the sounds of glasses clinking. When Linh sees the American, her first thought is of Ha Long. The American doesn't stand with the others. Like one of Ha Long's islets, he stands alone, to the side. He reminds her of rocks and water, treachery and beauty. He holds a glass of wine by its stem, then takes a sip.

She is wearing her green ao dai, berry-red flowers embroidered into a background of celadon, the cloth-covered clasps carving a half-circle across one side of her bodice. She studies language and speech, all the rules and symbols, sounds, but when she sees him, the words abandon her.

He sets the goblet down on a nearby table, and she walks over to where he stands, picks up his glass and presses it to her lips. She can feel his discomfort, taste it in the wine, that there is another woman between them. He hesitates for a moment, but finally speaks.

He doesn't like parties.

She likes his brevity with words, the way he is familiar with faltering.

Suddenly, her words return. She tells him the story of Ha Long, and as she does, she sails with him there, navigates its glassy waters. He listens carefully and he offers her a pact. They will go to Ha Long one day, he promises, when the war is over.

When will it be over?

That night, Linh dreams of Ha Long's sky, the way it winds around the earth and sea. She dreams of Cat Ba Island, its forests and mangrove trees, white-headed monkeys leaping along the limestone escarpments. She dreams of the caves, hollow and dark beneath the surface, and then she dreams of him, the American, and his promise to take her there.

Lucy

My father's study was a temple in our house, an island. It was his sanctuary, a place where he escaped my mother, Evelyn, and me, for hours at a time. Like yellow police tape, his closed door meant: Do not cross, do not enter.

Dad had bought the two-story house while on one of his leaves from Vietnam. It was part of a new tract of housing on Woodcliff Road in the hills of Sherman Oaks where he and some other doctors he knew had purchased quarter-acre lots. The development was carved like steps into the hillside and wound its way slowly up to Mulholland Drive. The study, too, was a room of steps, lined with floor-to-ceiling bookcases of encyclopedias, library-sized atlases, medical books, volumes on philosophy and psychology, books about World War II and Vietnam, and stacks of medical journals along three walls. Everything was neat, even the one remaining wall. It was filled with the photographs I'd enlarged in the closet Dad had converted into a darkroom for me. With time, and the little earthquakes that rolled through, the small, almost imperceptible tremors and settling of the house, they became crooked, but he always straightened them up.

It was the fall of 1977 in Los Angeles, the black asphalt streets were melting into the jelly of another valley Indian summer. The one Liquid Amber tree in front of the house defied the seasonless palms and the evergreen pines, blazing red on the hillside of ivy. A shaft of its light found the window of the study and cut a path onto the mahogany desk that filled up the room. Big as it was, the desk seemed to lay prostrate, unbalanced, under the weight of a thick, glass cover. A brass, pull-chain lamp topped with two milky-green lampshades illuminated the shiny surface. On one side, bills were piled tidy, addressed and stamped, ready for the mailman, on the other, another stack of medical journals, a silver letter opener resting nearby.

Dad loved his books, his papers. When he finished reading an article in a journal, he carefully wrote his initials on the upper right hand corner to signify completion; A.F. for Aaron Freedman. Sometimes, he underlined passages and cut out articles, putting them away into folders, but he always circled his signature, sealing it up. Another door closed.

His door was open today, and I walked in on him just as he shut the bottom, right-hand drawer of his desk. He locked it with a tiny key and put the key in his pants pocket.

"I haven't done enough today," I heard Dad say to himself, as if time was an enemy to be reckoned with, as though it could only be conquered by exhausting it, using it up to its very limitations. All Dad's lists, his items checked off, and his accomplishments, seemed to be part of his many atonements for others of his family, the ones whose time had been cut short, felled by history.

"Going out now, Lucy. You can read here—if you want to," Dad offered, knowing I liked to read in his study.

Dad always spoke in a kind of shorthand, little sentences cut into tiny pieces. I didn't know whether his words were spare because of the years he'd been a surgeon giving out orders in the operating room or whether it was because of the stutter he'd battled and over-come as a teenager.

"Thanks."

A month ago, on my fifteenth birthday, Dad had told me I could come in and read whenever he was out. It was his other pen-ance, to me this time, for the hours he kept his door shut. He'd said

I could borrow his books, anything except the ones about World War II and Vietnam. When I'd asked him why not those books, he'd changed the subject on me and I never got my answer...

"I'm leaving for the hospital, Evie," he called out to my mother. Even though he had his own practice, he remained on call at Northridge Hospital two days a week.

He picked up the car keys on the desk and started to walk out of the study. I stood at the doorway, and he stopped to give me a quick kiss on the forehead. Tall, his head almost reached the top of the threshold, and he seemed at home there, in a doorway, ready to make an exit.

"Lucy?"

"Yes?" I looked up at him, and it was as though he was about to say something else to me, but then changed his mind.

"See you later."

After I heard his car driving off, I closed the door and pushed it in all the way, made sure the handle clicked completely into the doorjamb.

His room was mine now, just like when I closed the door of my darkroom. I wished I was there now, but it was too hot in the house to do any printing today. A year ago, Dad had bought me all the equipment: a 35-millimeter camera and an Omega enlarger and an easel, chemical solutions and trays. At first, it was shooting film and the camera itself that fascinated me—the idea of appropriating an image, but it was in the darkroom that I did my best work. It didn't take me long to master standard printmaking, and I wasn't satisfied with its precise recordings. I soon found ways to diffuse the focus, control the developer and stop baths so as to blend images, block and mask them, turn the story in the photograph inside out. I experimented with negative prints and collage, multiple exposures and solarization. I mostly took photographs of TV images, and then reversed the tones, robbing them of their essence, and twisting them further into strange dreamscapes. There was beauty in the wordless gyrating patterns and texture, all the tonal gradations of gray. I wasn't interested in what was real—it was the resemblance to reality, its echo, that spoke to me.

It was cool in Dad's study, the air-conditioning unit purred in the window and I turned on the TV in the corner of the room. It didn't matter what was playing, I just wanted it on, a presence, the sound of it a safety net to catch me if I fell. I liked the way it tamed an image, framed it, the way it too mimicked reality.

Last night, the Fonz was on Channel Seven.

These *Happy Days* are yours and mine.

Like a dolls' house, the Cunningham's living room had pressed up against the TV screen. A salesman came and talked Mr. C. into building a bomb shelter. Everyone laughed when Mrs. Cunningham came running into the living room from the kitchen.

Ar-thur.

Mrs. C. was the only one who called the Fonz by his real name, Arthur.

I looked at the desk and sat down on Dad's wide, leather chair, opened the top drawers, pulling them all the way out. Each drawer was painstakingly arranged; stamps in a small plastic box, paper clips in another and envelopes bound by size with a thick rubber band. In the lower left drawers, there were neat folders with handwritten tabs designating household files and the articles he'd cut out.

Then I tried to open the bottom, right-hand drawer. I'd seen him lock it, but I shook the handle anyway. There were secrets in that drawer, I imagined, but it remained fixed and I took Dad's thin letter opener to pry the tiny lock open. I'd seen it done on television once, but it didn't work when I tried it, and I soon gave up.

Shutting the other drawers I'd opened, I left the desk and spread myself out on the floor with the encyclopedia. I opened it up and copied my favorite Japanese woodblocks, traced the women in colorful kimonos and intricate *obi* sashes onto onionskin paper. Shiny-smooth, their black hair stood high, prettily held in place with ivory hair combs, and I could almost hear their feet pad down rice-papered hallways. I chose another volume and sank into the lush of Dad's jade-colored carpet, and read about the excavation of the pyramids, walking through the tombs of the pharaohs, their maze of underground chambers. I felt the grooves of the hieroglyphics on the walls. Then I took out a couple of the books Dad didn't want me to read.

Suddenly, I was cold and I moved to the one spot on the carpet where the sun still blazoned a triangle of light through the window. I read a chapter from one book, then the other, and what I read spun together in my head. My Lai jumbled with Dachau, Kristallnacht with Tet.

I shut off the air-conditioning and fell asleep, the sound of the TV in the background.

I dreamed I was walking down a corridor of mirrors, a hallway of apparitions. Suddenly, I was in a wood of bare trees, and there were black dogs, snarling, snapping at my feet. In a clearing, there was a train, a cortege of boxcars full of human cargo, the sound of boots on leaves.

White, stenciled lettering flew past and I was on the train.

Ugly words.

They cut deep, like a blade.

The train raced faster and faster, until, plummeting off a cliff, it dissolved and fell into another terrain, wet and murky, a field of rice, but it was all the same, the clear, cold of blighted trees, the impressions of muddied waters. Two different landscapes collided and merged, blackened smokestacks raining human ash, grasslands of mist. I awoke just before the train slammed into the ground, my heart pounding, and the ground rose up to receive me.

Lucy

Later that night, Dad leaned over my bed to say goodnight. I could tell something was different about him. He looked thinner to me, his color gray, like newspaper print rubbed out in the rain. I felt it in the way he touched me. It seemed as though there was someone between us when he brushed aside my hair to kiss my cheek.

I took a long bath and then tried to fall asleep, but I heard every tiny noise, the water filling up in the icemaker in the refrigerator downstairs, and the 101 Freeway, a couple of miles away, its hum of cars like a far off river in the night. Then I heard my parents arguing again, and their voices wound around my head like the wet towels I'd dropped on the bathroom floor. I was used to their skirmishes, the private ground war between them.

My mother slammed her bedroom door shut and came out into the hallway. A minute later, Dad opened it and called out to her.

"Please come back to bed," he pleaded.

"No, Aaron." She was crying by the stairs.

I could hear him walk down the corridor to find her. I felt his presence on the other side of my wall, in the hallway, his tallness bending down to wrap in my mother, wearing down her defenses.

"Come on, Evie. It's late."

I sensed her fighting off his cocoon, fearing it, and yet the roundness of it, its heartbeat, so familiar to her.

Then I heard them returning to their room, the sounds of their bed, the mattress and box spring finding each other, rubbing against one another. They were the smallest of sounds too, but I heard their persistence.

I was still awake when Mom came to my bedroom to check on me later on. She looked pretty in her pink negligee and matching robe. It drifted behind her on the shag carpet, the slit of light from her bedroom lighting up the back of her head. I closed my eyes and pretended to sleep. She smelled good when she sat on my bed, making herself small, taking up only a fraction of the space, and I wanted her to stay, but he called out to her again from the other room to come back to bed, and his voice was anxious. He wanted her again and she was his, as she'd always been, and she was a slip of mercury, skidding away, never mine.

"Sleep tight, Lucy," she said, sounding wistful, and closed the door. Mom was in on my secret—she knew I had trouble falling asleep, about all the nights I'd walk around the house, switching on lights, turning on the TV. Sometimes, I wanted to tell Dad about not being able to fall asleep, about all the dreams I'd been having, but I didn't want him to know. It was an unspoken agreement between us, our decision not to tell him: It wouldn't be right somehow—a doctor who specialized in sleep disorders with a daughter who couldn't sleep. It wasn't hard keeping it from him. He was often away at night, and the times he was home, I made sure to stay quietly in my room.

I read for an hour, then switched off the lights.

I could never remember my dreams exactly.

Tunnels with no edges, rivers running away from mountains.

Nothing seemed to stay the same in the dreams. It was a universe turned upside down. Places were exchanged, like television channels switching from one station to the next. I shouted, but I couldn't speak out loud. People I didn't know seemed like memories, twinges, nagging at me. Once, blades whirled wildly in the sky, a line of people clinging to one another as they stood one up against each other on ladder rungs, like shells on an ammunition belt. There were colors I'd never seen before, walls of red and green, ochre and pink. There was one, small face, irresistible. In an instant, she disappeared, as though someone had thrown a rock at her watery reflection, and I melted into her skin.

The dreams made no sense, had no chronology. I didn't remember when I started having trouble sleeping or when the dreams began. I didn't have them every night, but when I did, I walked in and out of them, as if I couldn't make up my mind about letting them in or keeping them away. I'd sleep a little, then dream a bit, sleep again. But when I'd wake up, I'd remember only pieces of them, like torn-off corners of photographs.

I heard my parents' door open once again. "I have something to show you downstairs," Dad said. He was whispering this time. "Come with me."

I heard them go down the stairs and I waited, then followed after them in the dark.

In the kitchen, Dad lit a candle and I could smell the sulfur as the match ignited. Mom's eyes were closed, but her face seemed to light up with only the thought of the candle's solitary illumination. They fluttered open for a moment, but he brought his hands to her eyelids and gently closed them. He took her hand and they went to the living room, the candle flickering shadows on the wall. She was still wearing the thin, almost see-through robe, but the negligee was gone, and beneath, she too seemed transparent as shallow water.

He continued to whisper to her, just above her ear, at the soft indentation of her temple, leading her around the furniture. I could see she trembled, as they lingered in parts of the room, like stops on a train. He moved again, and the flame trailed a fume of black smoke.

"We're the same. We know how to survive, Evie," he said to her.

"It's not enough just to survive," her voice defied him and she opened her eyes.

He unlatched a window, pulled it open, and the night seeped in with the sound of a solitary airplane. It rose and fell as if in a trajectory, the noise of its engines both swallowed and magnified by the clouds that crept into the valley from the ocean all through the night.

"But we understand each other, you and I. Some people only have their enemies to defeat. We've had to overcome ourselves."

"I know," she capitulated.

They continued to talk to each other, but I didn't understand what they were saying now. Like code on a walkie-talkie, their words were gibberish, phrases sewn and spliced together to confound the foe.

"Evelyn."

Dad never called her by her given name, only "Evie," and she stopped abruptly.

"I don't want to hear you say it."

"Come on, you know it doesn't mean anything after all this time."

"It does."

"I won't say it then," he promised, and he fell silent, stepping back.

"You know I don't want you to go," she said quietly.

"I have to."

The house was warm and they continued walking together, opening all the windows, as if each one was a new port of call, a consolation for some journey they could not take together. She wanted to hurry on to the next, but he held her back, steadying her, sinking her.

"Slow down, Evie."

"I can't. There's so much I've missed."

Suddenly I was tired, spent. Quietly, I grabbed Dad's leather jacket from the hall closet and picked up the spare car keys in the kitchen. Out on the street, all the houses were dark except one, the lights all on, the blinds open in the dining room. Behind the large table, a mural took up the entire wall, painted-on gates and stairs leading to a fake ocean of blue.

I'd done it once before, taken the car and driven away without anyone knowing. I didn't have a learner's permit yet, but Dad had started to teach me how to drive. I had to get away now from them, from all the pretty houses up in the hills, the showy bougainvillea and lawns of ivy. It was the haze of the basin below, the giant crater bordered on one side by the Santa Monica Mountains, the Santa Susannas on the other that was drawing me in. Mom's car was parked on the street and I unlocked it, then got into the driver's seat, turning on the ignition.

It only took a few minutes to reach the flats. Soon, I found myself below the freeway, where the 405 and the 101 intersected above, and I felt the weight of the interchange rumbling over me, like gravity, the mass of a thousand cars, pressing. I was on Sepulveda, the fire station on my left, three lanes charging northward into the belly of the valley, its concave center, but I drove slowly, taking in the darkened auto parts stores and gas stations, storage warehouses and motor lodges—leftovers from the forties and fifties—tiny, strange enclaves with bright-red soda machines, AAA maps on wire racks. A truck rattled up from behind, honked at me, then passed me on the left.

I parked the car near the neon-blue sign of the Cabana Motel, but its name belied its collection of shabby bungalows. I craned my neck over the steering wheel to see more, but there were no cabanas, not even a pool in sight. All the numbered doors were shut, and I closed my eyes imagining the rooms of indistinguishable drapes, the identical beds and night tables.

Here too I was nothing but an interloper, peeping, looking in.

I drove around for a while then headed back home. Part way up Woodcliff, I noticed the mailboxes. Each house had a box by the curb, half cylinders sitting atop poles. They were all different, some intricate and ornate, others simple, like clan totems, omens, but I hated that they were all shut, and I rolled down my window and drove up the wrong side of the street, stopping to unfasten each box, and flip them open. I parked the car back in the same spot Evelyn had left it and looked back. The mailbox doors were all ajar now, freed of their riddles, hanging down like wide tongues.

Mom and Dad were still downstairs talking on the sofa when I returned home. I looked at them, my mother, her legs folded in, Dad wrapped around her like an envelope. A small gift box lay open on the coffee table.

I'd been out driving for an hour, but they hadn't even noticed I'd been gone.

I went straight up to my room and closed the door, left them to their strange journey together, their own sleeplessness, two magnets, positive and negative, repelling and pulling toward each other.

Lucy

A few days later, Mom took me with her to Laurel's Nails. I looked at the photographs on the walls. They were all of hands, perfect hands. No blue veins showed, not even a birthmark. They were marble-white, statues. There were images of nails dipped in color, pale and oval-shaped, burnished like tiny moons. There were long nails, stuck with tiny gemstones, painted with miniature landscapes, strange birds. The hands looked as though they were wings, about to take flight.

It all seemed like so much time and effort, so much work, for just a pair of hands.

Mom was already seated, but I was still standing by the front door.

"Here, sit right next to me, Lucy," she said, trying to rein me in.

"All right," but I didn't move. We were at the Vietnamese salon where she had an appointment every Thursday afternoon. I didn't usually like going out with Evelyn. It wasn't the same as an outing—with Dad, to his office on Ventura Boulevard, or when he made his rounds at Northridge Hospital. Mom didn't go out much.

She never came along with us on the trips I took with Dad to Catalina Island. She wouldn't even go with us to the football games at the Rose Bowl, the long palms fanning the rose above the stadium entrance like attendants. Dad said Mom didn't like to travel, hated boats. She wouldn't take the freeway, and only drove the surface streets that crisscrossed the San Fernando Valley. She didn't drive far—to the supermarket on Ventura Boulevard, her hairdresser in Tarzana—no place interesting.

But I liked the salon. There was something about this place, something different about my mother when she was here, a rivalry she was searching for in the reflections on the walls of mirrors. I looked her way. She had a perfect mouth, a flame of red in her hair.

I walked over to where she was sitting…

It was also one of the few places I could doze off. There and the Bullocks store, when Mom would go off to buy a sweater and I'd sneak off sometimes to the mattress department and find a bed to curl up into. The salespeople never chased me away. I don't know how long I'd sleep like that, but for some reason Mom always knew where to find me.

"Come on, honey," she said, and the word "honey" should have come out of her mouth sleepy, sticky-sweet, but instead it was impatient. "How about a manicure today, Lucy?" Mom asked me. Now she was trying hard to sound cheerful and I knew she was covering something up.

I wasn't too sure why she always came here. There were other places to get manicures, American places and I'd thought she didn't like anything that reminded her of Vietnam. She hadn't even seemed to like Doan, the Vietnamese girl Dad used to bring over to our house when I was ten.

But all I said was "maybe later." I decided I wasn't going to give her a hard time today. I knew I could be stubborn. The more someone told me not to do something, the more I wanted to do it. Like the time Dad took me to the gardens at the Huntington. We went to the hot house where there were hundreds of different kinds of cactus, beautiful shapes bubbling out of the terra cotta pots. The sign said not to touch the plants, but all I'd wanted to do was reach out to them, feel the prick of their spines and thorns.

"Well then, just sit next to me," Mom said. She sat down at Rose's station and pulled a chair close, putting her purse beneath, as if we were about to go on a trip together. "He's going to tell you. He wants to tell you himself, but I wanted you to know, to be prepared."

"Know what?" I asked. It wasn't unusual for Evelyn to start speaking, mid-sentence, without a beginning, sometimes without an end.

"He's going back to Vietnam."

It had been four years since the last time Dad had been in Vietnam. "Dad's going back? But the war is over."

"Son of a bitch," she inhaled, as if she'd taken a quick drag of a cigarette. "He should never have left us to go there in the first place. I thought it was done with by now, but it's happening all over again. It's never going to be over," she said, exhaling now.

I was about to ask her what she was talking about when I heard Rose call out.

"Anybody know him?" Rose addressed the room. She was the manicurist closest to the door, and she controlled the buzzer that had been installed just after the salon had been robbed. She pointed her chin in the direction of the entrance and poised her index finger over the buzzer.

I too looked toward the front.

There was a man on the other side of the tinted glass. He brought his face up to the glass and his nose became wide and flat.

The salon was full, a woman in each of the ten manicure stations set in two neat rows, but no one responded. Gooseneck lamps arched hot over each of the stations. The manicurists hunched over their clients' hands as if they were sewing fabric. Near the TV set, there was a wall-clock that was twenty minutes slow.

"Anyone—?" Rose asked again. Her name really wasn't Rose, she'd once explained to Mom, it was Thu, but in America, she called herself Rose.

It was easier to be Rose, easier for the Americans, she'd explained. Americans didn't like to struggle over a name.

A few of the women having pedicures looked up lazily, but no one seemed to know the man and Rose shrugged, took her finger off the button, went back to filing Evelyn's nails.

The man rapped on the door a couple more times, but Rose ignored him. He smiled, but then walked away.

I liked this place, the idea of a place for women only, where men had to be buzzed in, given permission to enter, as if it were holy, sacred, like Dad's study.

I watched Rose work on my mother's hands. Her black hair was parted in the middle and I could see the salt-white of her scalp as she worked.

"You soak now."

She guided my mother's right hand into warm, soapy water, and cradled her left hand in her own. Rose used three straight strokes back and forth with the file, then set it down to hunt for a different emery board. She found it in the back of one of the little drawers of the manicure station.

I felt my own hands grow limp. Maybe it was the fumes of the pinkish acrylic powders, the whirring buffers, or the sound of General Hospital on the television hanging like a painting on the back wall. Maybe it was only the water bubbling, percolating or watching Rose's strong hands massaging Evelyn's fingers across the knuckles, then her wrists and forearm until I couldn't tell which hand was my mother's and which was Rose's.

Rose continued to massage Mom's hands while talking to another one of the manicurists. I didn't understand what Rose was saying, but her words jumped up and down, vibrated into the air like tiny gongs.

Rose had delicate lashes above her white mask, the same kind of mask Dad used to wear when he was a surgeon. Evelyn always said that Dad had the hands of a surgeon. I looked down at my own. They seemed insignificant in comparison.

"You forgot to chose your color," Rose reprimanded gently.

Mom leaped up in a blur and snapped up the first bottle off

the neat row of polishes on the glass shelf. She always seemed to be in a hurry, breathless, as though she were making up for stillness. She handed me the bottle instead of Rose, and I looked at the bottom label. Mango. It was also the color of the shrine of fruit and incense near the water cooler in the back of the salon.

I gave the bottle to Rose and she unscrewed the top off the bottle. It was too thick and Rose frowned, then poured a drop of acetone into it and shook the bottle up and down. Afterward, she applied the first coat to the fingers of Mom's right hand.

My eyelids were getting heavy.

Just then, the man who'd tried to come in before reappeared at the door. This time, he wore white gloves, like a mime. He grinned and waved his hands around. Everyone in the salon was looking at him now. He put his hands on the sidewalk and stood in a handstand. Jumping back up, he took a deep bow from behind the glass. Then he took out a handmade sign from his trouser pocket and unfolded it, held it up to the window.

Palm Reader.

The Future in Your Hand.

"Oh, let him in," someone yelled out from the back of the salon. "He's all right."

Rose reluctantly buzzed him in.

"Ladies," he cooed. He had a buttery face, long, thin hands. "Who'd like their palm read first? How about you," he said, reaching over to touch my mother's wrist.

"No." Rose slapped his hand away. "You don't know anything," she said to him, holding on to my mother's hand. "You go over there." She ordered him off to the back of the salon.

"Don't you want your palm read?" I asked Mom, rubbing my eyes.

"Men don't know anything about the future, right Rose?" my mother asked.

There seemed to be an unspoken understanding between them, and Evelyn looked to Rose, waited for her to nod in agreement. "Your mother, she's right," Rose said, then started on a second coat of color. Rose dabbed the brush into the vial. She began at the bottom of the nail, right up at the arc of the cuticle, then covered the nail in three, quick brush strokes. She scraped off any excess with her thumbnail and wiped it on a paper towel.

"What do you mean?" I asked.

"Woman, she hold the future in her belly," Rose said pointed to her stomach and then clicked off the overhead light. She turned on a small, plastic fan. "A man, he don't know anything like that."

Mom got up quickly and almost lost her balance.

Rose reached out to catch her.

"You wait this time," Rose said to Mom. "Not hurry out, like last time."

"Okay, okay," my mother surrendered, sitting back down, as if she'd come home, found her equilibrium.

Rose aimed the fan toward Mom's fingers.

"You wait. You wait for your daughter to sleep," Rose said.

I closed my eyes and saw shadows of light filtering through dark shutters, colored tiles and bundles of silk. I heard the noises of an open market, and insects in the trees. I felt the cold of stone, long-necked storks and swimming tortoises carved in relief.

Mai

I wasn't surprised when Van told us we would have to leave. I'd known Luong didn't like my pretty mother going out to the streets with Van every day. Luong was always needling Van, telling him they had enough mouths to feed. She didn't like me or my mother.

Bastard child.

A child without a father is like a house without a roof, Luong enjoyed repeating.

She didn't know I was not even a house, I was a wall half-built, but I couldn't let her find out.

"Linh is no good at selling pancakes. She stands there as if she was a queen, only pretending to be crazy when it suits her. She's no better than a lump of cold rice," Luong continued her campaign against us.

Van didn't want to listen to his wife. I knew he treasured his snatched looks at Linh's delicate face—his opportunity to be alone with her—but Luong finally found his ear.

"We don't have enough room for the three of you," Van said early one morning, shaking his head. "Maybe you'll have to go."

Luong smiled, thinking she'd won, but Thanh knew exactly

what to do. She took Van aside and began her peddling. She reminded Van of old debts; the job Grandfather had found him when the Americans were here, driving foreigners around Saigon in one of Grandfather's own Mercedes. And at the end of all her negotiating and persuasions, the hard looks she flung at Luong, it was decided that I would replace Linh. I would now help Van sell his pancakes on the street instead of her. Thanh had suggested an attractive exchange: Van would have his help and Luong could keep her eye on Linh.

"Mai will do it," Thanh said, cementing the deal.

That same morning, I went out with Van. I didn't like him or the smell of the dark oil on his cart, but I didn't mind being out on the street. After a short while, I knew my way around the city, learned every alley and back way, the crumbling tunnels underneath Ho Chi Minh City. I knew all the old colonial buildings, the ones left over from the French. I explored the red brick Notre Dame Cathedral and the post office, where I'd hide under a wooden bench and look up at the iron and glass ceiling. Built by Gustave Eiffel, the plaque said, and there was something about the Frenchman's black iron, the thought of his girders, that filled me up, and gave me strength.

There were other children like me on the streets, strange-looking children with light-colored hair or dark skinned and kinky-haired. They begged in the streets, and sold postcards and playing cards with dirty pictures. People stopped and called them names, but I was different.

No one dared to stare at me. I was almost as tall as Van, and my eyes were green like the river. I knew just how to make the right expression, not like the others, their beggar's looks. I knew they wouldn't buy noodle *pho* from the old man on the corner. I knew I could make them buy their pancakes from me, the dragon-eyed one. Van soon realized I was his lucky charm, bringing him new customers.

And I was useful in other ways. I could hear trouble, police whistles from far off. Sometimes, they'd come around for no reason and overturn our cart, but I gave Van a signal, and he packed up the stove and oil in an instant. After that, he patted me on the head and never let Luong complain about Linh or me again.

Linh now stayed at home all day, not going out. There were times when she slept for days without waking up.

One afternoon, I came back to give her the few extra coins I'd hidden away from Van, but she was asleep, spread out like water spilled on the floor. She took up the entire space that was set aside for the three of us. She took it over as if it were hers to be taken, as though all sleep and all space belonged to her, only her.

I wanted to give her the coins, and I shook her awake, pressed the coins in her hand.

"Wake up, Linh."

"Leave me alone, let me sleep," she growled at me.

"I want to hear about the words," I said, trying to entice her away from her sleep. "Tell me about them."

She stirred, then opened her eyes.

"Why are they so important?" I asked.

She cupped her hands around the coins. Her voice was hollow, like a husk. "Without words, there is no humanity. We are mere beasts without them. It is the words, language, that separate us from the animals; they give us the train fare for the journeys in our dreams."

I looked around Van's apartment, the walls still pockmarked by gunfire. Outside, the streets bore the remnants of the war, burned out tanks and shattered glass that no one had replaced yet. Linh was wrong. We were beasts in spite of our words—because of them; I let her go back to sleep, her haven.

I watched her for hours, watched how her sleeping fits, her spasms, would melt into a candied sleep. She became all sugar and soft and I knew she was dreaming of her American again by the way her legs gave in to the sticky mat on the floor.

I took over then, like I always did. I'd become a smuggler, sneaking dreams across borders. I'd sell pancakes during the day, but at night, I had my other vocation—taking what was mine from Linh.

❧

Linh and her American take a cab to Tan Son Nhut Airport. She looks out the back of the sooty cab window.

There is a Pan Am sign on the other side of the road.

Welcome to Sunny Saigon.

The airport is teeming with people, planes flying in and out, one right after the other. There are cargo planes, their bellies full of equipment, troops and tanks. On the tarmac, there is a jumble of crates, strewn luggage.

From the air, Linh sees the rows of corrugated roof shanties, the shacks made of soda cans that have sprung up around Saigon.

Goodbye Saigon.

He takes her for a week to Paris, to a little hotel on the Left Bank. The room is small, barely enough for the bed and a desk, but she likes its smallness, its enclosure, like a pen. He could have taken her somewhere closer, to Hong Kong, or Tokyo, Hawaii, to the places the officers and doctors take their wives, lovers for a week of R&R, some respite from the war. But he wants to go far away.

He insists on Paris.

Linh has been to Paris before. Grandfather has taken her there many times to the Georges V Hotel on the Champs Elysees, but she tells her American it is her first time to please him.

She wants him to be happy in his audacity.

She lets him take her to the Eiffel Tower and the Sacré Coeur, a boat ride down the Seine. She pretends she's never seen the willful spires of Notre Dame, the river that flows below their hotel window, the bridges that arch like the backs of women across the water. He wants to be her teacher and read the guidebook out loud in front of the Louvre, pointing out the history of its architecture, the perspectives; she lets him.

The evenings are cool, but she keeps the windows open all night while they make love. It isn't the moonlight or the air she craves. It is a different breeze she wants—the remnants of the gusts that flow off the city's monuments, their cold, foggy whiteness.

He falls asleep and she knows something is amiss. He's been here before—with her. He's made some kind of exchange, as if a word has been replaced, thrown, upsetting the unique balance of a sentence.

Then she understands. She is the word, the name that has been swapped, mutated.

I'm not Evelyn.

I am not Eve-lyn.

I'm not half of her. I am a whole.

I am Linh.

Still, she loves Paris, wants to stay on with him. He belongs to her there. She has him all to herself in Paris. There is no triage, no hospitals, no helicopters to take him away for days at a time.

He takes Linh to a little shop on the Rue du Bac. There is barely a counter in front of the old jeweler. He buys her a gold ring and she wears it on her left hand, content in their pretense, the mischief of its fit.

Bonjour Monsieur, Bonjour Madame, the concierge at the hotel smiles.

They take a taxi to the Eiffel Tower and they ride the elevator to the top. Above the fog, her head suddenly clears. She drops words like gems from the tower—

Soon though, he wants to cut the trip short. He suddenly itches to go back, to return to the deltas. He misses the gummy air, blood on his hands. His fingers tingle with an ache for his scalpel and sutures, his surgeon's silky threads. He wants to go back where adrenaline pumps in his veins, where his hands perform miracles.

She understands.

She's been with him there, in Saigon—the place he'd run away to, away from his wife, his refuge. It is in Paris where she understands how it is to be his wife, to be like her, cut away from him like the bullets and shrapnel he extracts.

They leave the city the next day, but she already knows. She can feel it inside of her, in every limb, every part, on the tips of her fingers, the palm of her hand—the child they've made in Paris.

Mai

After a few months on the streets, I learned how to snatch an orange off the back of a bicycle or cart. There wasn't even much of a challenge to it. I was quick like the crazy street magician. He clapped and made white birds disappear, coins fall from the sky. He ordered ropes to untangle. He was crazier than Linh, but his hands were steady and quick, like the hands of Linh's American. I'd seen them in Linh's dreams, seen how he cut through flesh and bone, and pried his way into blood and tissue.

I studied the street merchants. There was Do, the barber. His clients sat on a crate while he propped a cracked mirror against a wall for them. Quickly, he snipped away with his scissors, then applied a touch of scented hair oil. Then there was Tho, who crushed sugar cane, and Bui, who repaired bicycle tires, patched them and filled them up with air. I watched them closely, learned their secrets.

The items I took were not important, just bits, things other people had forgotten, lost things. I found a book, a battered English dictionary, and brought it back to Linh one evening. There were pages torn out, but I thought she'd like to hold a book, see her words again.

Linh took the book from me, felt its tattered spine, and rubbed the thinning pages between her fingertips.

"See," she pointed to a page. "Every word is a relationship to something other than itself, it's a derivation, a variation," she said as though she was back in a classroom among wooden chairs and blackboards, and she seemed content.

Then I took out a ring I'd found. I hoped she'd like the gold ring someone had left in the washroom of the Continental Hotel…I put it in a box, and wrapped it up in paper, but she pushed it away.

Why did you wear his ring but not mine? You were never his wife.

Thanh came into the room. She immediately noticed the box and wrapping paper.

"What do you have there?"

"Nothing."

I stuffed the ring in my pocket and Thanh put her hand out.

"It's your duty to give it to me."

"No," I said, and I took the ring out again and held it up in the air to taunt her.

"Some girls know their obligations. The Lady Ly Thi Thien knew her duty. Bethothed to a poor peasant who had been sent off to fight in a war, she was unwilling to accept the advances of a powerful man. Rather than betray her true love, she threw herself over the cliff of Black Lady Mountain."

"Where is Black Lady Mountain?" I asked.

"A long way from here," Linh suddenly spoke up.

I looked at Linh, her tiny hands, the blue veins that traveled like brooks to her wrist.

"Is that what you want Linh to do—to find the Black Lady Mountain and throw herself down?" I challenged Thanh.

"No. The mountain has already found her."

"What do you mean?"

"Every woman has her own Black Lady Mountain," Thanh said.

I thought of the mountain and it rose in my head, like a slow eruption, and I held on tighter to the ring. Then I looked at Linh again, and I became weak. Thanh saw her opportunity, snatching the ring from me…

I ran out of the apartment to the street.

Behind a doorstep, there was a broken doll and. I picked it up. The doll had a pretty face, like Linh, but its limbs were gone. I'd repaired things before, Van's radio, and the stove. I knew how to take things apart and put them back together, but I knew I couldn't fix the doll, just like I couldn't fix Linh.

What good was a pretty doll to someone like me?

Thanh always said I acted like a boy.

I looked down the block. It was full of boys. There was no effort in the easy way they sat and crouched and climbed, their skinny arms and scraped knees, their idle hands. Except for Van, we were all women, Linh, Thanh and Luong, her child and me, and that was all I understood, the household of women.

Van was the only man I'd known. He strutted in his own home with license, but on the street he jumped at every unexpected noise. He yelled at Luong, but cried when she scolded him.

I'd only heard the stories of other men, and they were phantoms to me. Grandfather had abandoned us in death, and Linh's American couldn't be trusted to come back, to return to those who waited. Neither had a woman's hand.

The Black Lady Mountain knew that.

It wasn't love or duty that made the Lady throw herself off the mountain. It was betrayal.

I ran from Van's apartment, from Linh and Thanh. I fled to the Saigon River and stole into the wharf. On the river, the boats creaked softly in the water, rocked gently from side to side. In the sampans, the lanterns glowed with secrets in the labyrinth of waters. I found the coiled ropes that held the boats and unraveled them.

Thanh was wrong. I did know my duty—it was to untie the boats, free them from their moorings.

⁂

From the window of Grandfather's villa at night, Linh hears the air strikes on the villages outside the city. The Americans bring new sounds with them, terrible sounds—the sounds of helicopter blades and convoys, metal grinding against metal. There are the sounds of the howitzers exploding, firing their shells, while flashes of orange light up the night sky. She thinks of the word "howitzer," how the Dutch word for a sling makes its way from the fifteenth century to be reborn as a cannon.

The thick night swelters with the brightness of magnesium flares, hissing in the blackness, but she shivers, alone at the window. She puts her hands over her ears. It is on these nights that she feels it creeping, insinuating into her. It is a madness that comes and goes, and when it comes, it consumes her. Thanh has seen it too, its beginnings, and blames it on the American, but Linh knows better. It had nothing to do with him. She is born to it.

The melancholy is in her blood.

When daylight comes, the sounds are different, the noises of shopkeepers, awakening streets. Linh walks past the makeshift piles of Tampax, Prell shampoo and toilet paper that are sold on the street. She walks to Tan Hue, the Street of Flowers, where kiosks still bloom with orchids and gardenias. Out on the pony carts, there are piles of papayas and pineapples, mangos and guavas. The war has not yet come to the expensive shops of the Eden Arcade, to the tailor and fabric stores where they sell fine silks and elegant brocades. It hasn't invaded the apothecaries where the drawers are still full of herbs and roots, bark and dried powders. It hasn't darkened the pool, the lunches of the members of Le Cercle Sportif Club, tanning themselves in their bikinis and Speedos, flicking their gold, Dunhill lighters open.

She meets him at the café with the striped blue umbrellas. She sits down and he orders black coffee and a citron pressé for her, but he doesn't touch his cup. She tries to talk to him, but he doesn't hear her.

Don't hide behind your newspaper.

I'm tired, Linh. I don't want to talk now.

You never want to talk.

Sometimes I can't.

Suddenly, there is an explosion. It's a grenade, tossed, and people are strewn, bleeding, glass and twisted chairs everywhere.

He quickly begins to tend to the injured. She watches him move from one to the other, seeing who is alive, who is wounded. An ambulance arrives and he jumps in the back.

Go home, Linh. I'm going to be at the hospital all night. I want to come with you. Go home. Go to sleep. She hails a cab and follows the ambulance to the Third Field Hospital, not far from the airport.

Once a school, the hospital is painted white and built around a large courtyard. It has a main gate where ambulances bring the wounded in from a chopper pad.

When they arrive at the gate, he tells her to go home again, but Linh doesn't leave. She passes the mess hall on the first floor and the old school gym, which has been converted into living quarters.

She finds the operating room and waits there for the rest of the afternoon. It is a week before Christmas and the Third Field is decorated with red and green streamers, and there are cutouts of angels over the beds, but Linh only sees the cracked wall tiles falling with effort against each other.

One doctor hurries into the OR. Two nurses come by. Exhausted, they look like phantoms in white, their hands and uniforms bloodied after a twelve-hour shift.

When are they going to evacuate those poor bastards?

It doesn't matter. They're all going to die anyway.

Suddenly, they notice Linh.

"You can't stay here," they say in unison, but Linh doesn't move.

Like wind chimes, they rub against each other and whisper.

She's heard it before. It is the whispers of the donut dollies and the secretaries at the embassy.

You have him now, but he'll go home.

He'll go home to his wife.

❦

The Third Field is the only hospital in the city where the military nurses wear whites. For a moment, she wishes she could be one of them, that she could take on their whiteness, wear their buttons and epaulettes, the insignias on their collars. And when they stand in the operating rooms, they wear their gloves and gowns, surgical masks, and stand close to him. They piece things together, put them in the right place.

Maybe she could be good at mending flesh too.

She is good at mending words, reconstructing them.

47

Isn't it the same, words and flesh?

When night falls, he still hasn't come out of the OR *and a pink-blue gecko crawls from behind a makeshift sign tacked onto the wall. She walks over to the window. Out on the street, there are more signs, street signs and store signs, the letters melting into one another.*

They are in Roman letters.

It was a French Jesuit who did that, took the language, the heavenly Mon-Khmer, and made it quoc ngu. He tainted the chu nom, the Chinese characters, their delicate brush strokes and wings, twisted them straight, into a monkish Roman script. The cold of French, its logic, should never have tainted a language of single syllable words, of intuition, and ambiguity.

It is a tongue where names can be male or female.

They captured everything else. Why didn't they leave the language alone?

From behind the door of the operating room, Linh thinks she hears the American's voice and she pushes the door open. But it is only the air-conditioning unit. He is gone and there is only the gurgle of machines, the noise of the air tanks.

It is a wounded woman, rasping into an oxygen bag.

Lucy

I could hear Dad calling to me, but his voice sounded as though he was far away.

"Lucy, are you ready to go?"

I was in the darkroom, and almost finished with the prints I'd taken the other day. Once I got going in the darkroom, it was hard to get me to leave. The darkness was kind, and I was capable here, where the safelight was my only illumination. Sometimes, it felt as if I was recreating the scale of the world, interpreting it, manipulating its images.

"I'll be out in a minute."

Last week, I'd worked on something new. Instead of photographic paper, I'd tested out positive transparencies for printing. They were high contrast and eliminated all the middle tones, emphasizing only the blacks and whites. Elvis Presley had died in the summer and I'd taken photographs of his funeral directly off the television. It amazed me what the camera had caught in a fraction of a second, and what it hadn't captured: the illusion of mourning.

"Do you want to come for a ride with me to the office?" Dad

was on the other side of the door. He knew not to come in when I was printing.

I almost didn't want to go. Today, I was working on something new. I'd had a couple of shots leftover on the Elvis roll and I'd taken a photo of a homeless woman sleeping on a bench on Ventura Boulevard. I clicked off the bulb and looked at the image in the fixer solution. It was a straight print for once, no manipulation, but I liked the way the light played with the woman's face, how shadow crept into the recesses. It was as though she'd been transported on a path of light. I took out the print with a pair of tongs and placed it carefully in the washing tray. Normally, I would have taken the print out of the water to dry, but I wanted to experiment further, and see what leaving it in for the day would do to the print.

"Sure," I called out.

"After that I'll drop you off at your grandparents," he said, walking away.

I opened the door and went back to my room to get dressed. I yanked up the blinds, then looked out to see the sliver of the Santa Monica Mountain range barely visible above the treetops. It was Saturday, and Dad often dropped me off in the afternoons at my grandparent's house in West Hollywood. My grandmother Ruth would call mid-week and invite him to come over too, but he'd always decline. Lately, he seemed even more estranged from his parents, and I was their consolation prize, just like on *The Price is Right*.

We're sorry you won't be coming back next week, contestant number one. But we do have some wonderful parting gifts for you.

I liked tagging along with Dad to his office, though. It was there, when we were alone, that he talked to me about his most difficult cases.

"I need to pick something up. Actually, I want to see if I can find an article."

I didn't need an explanation, but he was always trying to explain, reason things out, as if every problem had a logical answer, a solution. It was as though problems for him were only words in a reference book, set out in columns, spelled out in boldface and precisely pronounced, the definitions at attention, ready to serve.

He should have known I'd have gone, no matter what.

I got dressed quickly and met him at the front door. Mom walked by and he grabbed her by the waist, kissed her on the mouth, hard, as if he was still making something up to her, trying to prove something, prove her wrong.

We walked out to the driveway together and he opened the car door for me. Then he bowed slightly and tipped an imaginary cap, like a chauffeur. I was too old for the game we used to play, but I didn't mind. I nodded and jumped into the back and waited for him to get into the driver's seat. Then I climbed up over the front seat to sit next to him.

Later, Dad parked in the back lot of the medical building where he rented office space. Carved into the blue tile was Caduceus, a wing-topped staff, wound about by two snakes, conjoined as one, the same insignia I'd once seen on Dad's old army uniform. The building had a small elevator, but his office on the second floor could be reached through the outdoor stairs and a balcony. We walked up the stairs and he unlocked the door. The blinds were shut tight.

"No patients coming in?" I asked, disappointed, as we went inside.

"Not today."

He turned on all the lights and smiled. He always seemed happiest when he was in his office and lab. The sleep lab looked more like a hotel room. It had a bed with sheets and blankets, pillows, and the walls were painted in soft colors. There were no overhead lights, the microphones and machines, the infrared camera hidden away.

Dad was one of the first specialists in sleep disorders in the country. He'd done research on sleep deprivation and light therapy after he'd left the army, spending time at Stanford, working in their sleep clinics. He liked to monitor his own patients and many times he'd come to the lab on weekends and stay up all night, observe, make notes about sleeping positions. He'd put sensors on a patient's head, face, chest, stomach, and legs, while his equipment recorded brain waves, eye movements, breathing, and heart rate, even muscle activity.

But even specialists in sleep medicine like Dad didn't understand everything about sleep, about why a person needed to sleep and dream. There were many explanations, but no good answers about why we human beings spend almost half our lives sleeping. Certain experts said dreams were part of the sleep cycle, a transfer of information between different parts of the brain.

I looked at Dad. He was at his best here, in his office, with his sleep data and research nearby, but he wasn't very talkative today, and he took out a case file from behind the reception desk, and started to scan the contents.

"Tell me again—about animals and sleep," I coaxed.

"Sleep is essential for all mammals and even some bird species," he said, still looking at the file.

"But dolphins are different, aren't they? I read about them in an article you gave me. They're able to sleep one hemisphere of their brain at a time, so they won't drown."

He looked up from the file and smiled at me.

"That's right."

"And then you said something else about dreaming," I said, continuing to engage him.

"Well, some people say that they're like condensers, squeezing experiences into a short period of time. What do you think?"

"Maybe dreams are reflections, like an image in a pool of water," I offered up my own unscientific explanation.

He thought for a moment. "I like that idea. The truth of the matter is that we still don't know," he said, putting away the file and taking out a book. "Can you keep yourself busy for awhile? I've got some work to do."

"Sure."

I looked at the freshly made up bed in the corner of the lab, and felt a yawn creep slowly up the back of my throat.

Dad had shown me how to work all the machines and whenever I visited him at the lab I usually played back the videotapes of the night before. Some people grabbed their pillows and ground their teeth. Others stayed in the same position for the entire night, others moved all over the bed. It wasn't difficult to tell when someone was dreaming, the way their eyelids fluttered when their eyes moved back and forth. The heart, brain, and breathing monitors jumped up and down and it was almost as if they were awake. It was strange watching someone sleep. I felt like an intruder when I'd hear them talk or moan, suddenly sit up in bed as if they were reliving something.

But I couldn't help myself and I slid in last night's tape.

The man started off quietly, his head burrowed under the pillow. After a while, he moved the pillow under his arms and wrestled with it. Later, he thrashed around, turned over onto his stomach and his arms flapped to the sides as if he were swimming. I wondered what Dad would say about this patient, what his diagnosis would be.

I yawned again and nodded off.

I was taking pictures, going from one room to the next in an unfamiliar house, a house with no doors. In each open doorway, I stood for a moment, then snapped a photograph, the camera melting away, the walls sliding in. A bulb glowed red over three yellow trays and images bubbled up, surfacing like divers from the heavy liquid. Black and white turned lacquer red, like rescue flares in the night.

"Are you all right?"

"Dad?"

I hadn't heard him come into the lab. Seeing Dad now, I felt suddenly awake, completely alert.

"Come on, I'm almost done here."

I stopped the tape and followed him to his office. His framed diplomas covered two of the walls. There were his medical school diplomas, his certificates and awards, photographs of him shaking hands with a couple of senators.

"Why aren't you a surgeon anymore?" I asked, testing him.

"I just don't have the hands for it anymore. They're not steady enough."

I looked at his large, sturdy hands. They were tree trunks, rooted, not a hint of a tremor. It couldn't have anything to do with them.

"That's what it means you know," he said, distracted.

"What 'what' means?"

"Surgeon. It's from the Greek. It means a person who works with the hands. Someone told me that."

"Who?"

"Someone I once knew."

I wished there'd been some patients this morning. I liked to see Dad at work. He'd take his time, asking them lots of questions, but he'd never look at them directly. Mom said he wasn't very good with people, that he'd been a surgeon so long that he was used to only treating patients under anesthesia, asleep, but his patients seemed to like and trust him. There were always baskets of fruits, bouquets of flowers on the receptionist's counter.

There was something changed about him today, a flame lit. He couldn't sit still, as if he'd found a new project, something he could sink his teeth into. I watched him as he went from one pile of books to another on the long bookcase behind his desk. In between the piles of medical journals, there were photographs of Mom and me.

"Here, this might be it," he said, sounding relieved. He picked up a book and was about to put a paper clip to mark a page, but then stopped. "No, that's not it, I'm wrong," he said to himself, then turned to me. "Lucy, I'm going away for a few weeks," he said in a rush, and the words "wrong" and "Lucy" seemed to spring out of the same sentence.

"Really?" I'd been waiting for him to tell me, but I pretended I didn't know. I'd been hoping Mom had been mistaken, that he might have brought me to the office to tell me that he was finally going to take me with him to one of his seminars. He'd been promising for months to take me, but he wasn't always very good at keeping promises.

"You be nice to your mom while I'm away," he continued. "She's going to need some extra attention."

I turned away from him, and made sure he didn't see my face.

Why me?

He expected me to make up for all the time he didn't spend with Mom, the late nights at the office, the board meetings at the hospital, his volunteer work.

"Y--your mother's—a special woman," he said.

"Sure," I said, but I was unconvinced.

I'd heard all the stories about Mom—about how she'd had

polio when she was a child—and how she'd spent a year in an iron lung. But that was a long time ago and I didn't see it. I didn't see how it made her special.

He put the books down for a moment. "It's going to be a long flight. I can't sleep on airplanes anymore. But when I was over there, I used to be able to sleep anywhere. Sometimes, I'd even fall asleep standing up. That's where I'm going, you know, back, to Vietnam."

Vietnam.

There it was, that word again—the place I'd seen on TV. Whenever I heard someone mention Vietnam, it was like a fire bell in my head. Dad hardly ever talked about Vietnam, but my mother did. She'd told me he hadn't been drafted and even after she'd begged him not to, he'd gone ahead and volunteered anyway.

I looked at Dad. He was still searching for that article.

"Can I help you?"

"No, no. It's O.K. I'll find it myself," he said. He was sitting on the floor now, looking at the bottom shelf of his bookcase.

Myself. It was as though he was shutting the door of his study.

૨૯

I suddenly remembered the portable television set Mom had bought one of the times Dad had been over in Vietnam. She kept adjusting the antenna, but she could never get the colors just right and the jungle always looked orange, the bamboo stalks yellow. Every Christmas, we watched the USO show aired from an Air Force carrier, or some giant hangar.

We're broadcasting to you live.

From somewhere in Vietnam, Bob Hope said, smiling and swinging his golf club. Then a longhaired blond in white go-go boots and a mini skirt came out and all the GI's yelled and whooped.

Ho Chi Minh Trail, Viet Cong, Da Nang, the Mekong Delta, Tet. I'd repeat the words Walter Cronkite said on the evening news. Once a week, white numbers flashed behind him on a black screen.

U.S. Dead.

U.S. Wounded.

I couldn't stop watching, but even so, Vietnam didn't seem real. The camera shook and dipped quickly from the sky to the ground. Helicopter blades always whirred, stirred the high grasses like waves. Soldiers wore green helmets camouflaged with leaves or wore bandanas, smeared their faces with black pitch. The sleeves of their uniforms were rolled all the way up their arms. Breathing hard, they carried the wounded on stretchers. Then they sat down to rest, have a smoke.

"Dad, can I get a TV for my room? Diane's father bought her a Sony with a remote."

When I'd sleep over at my friend's house we'd close the door of her bedroom and turn off the lights. The volume on low, the TV would flicker, the light bouncing off the walls. I'd half-hear the sounds.

He was still on the floor reading.

"It's not a good way of falling asleep, Lucy," he said closing the book he was holding. When he ended a sentence with my name, it usually meant the matter was settled.

He was wrong. Maybe he was a sleep specialist, but he didn't know everything about sleep. The TV was the best way to fall asleep, like having a fish tank in a room, my own tiny, illuminated world in the dark.

"How long are you going to be away?" I asked.

"About three weeks. Vietnam is very far, you know."

"I know."

I'd seen it on the map. So many times in his study, I'd taken out the atlas, found the page. I'd trace its outlines with my finger; follow the curves of the country, the lush of green. Somewhere under the twist of the rivers, the dark forests, the nipples of mountains, was my father's seduction, the reasons he kept going back.

Three long weeks alone with my mother.

I looked up at Dad and it seemed as if he was already gone.

But then I thought about the times Dad had been away in Vietnam. Mom had played checkers with me, read me stories in the bath. She'd even done handstands and rolled around on the floor with me. She was different when he wasn't around, and suddenly I wanted him to leave.

Go now. Don't go.

"Can't you stay?"

"No, I have to," he said, and it was the same "have to" I'd heard so many times before. His commitment to some important undertaking required my unquestioning obedience as well. He looked at his watch. "It was where I thought a lot about sleep," he said, changing the subject. "They called it sleep therapy then, for the guys who had combat fatigue. They'd sedate them, and then give them something to eat, sedate them again. They'd keep them under for three or four days. Then they'd send them back out to the field."

"What was it like, Dad?"

He paused for a long time before he answered.

"I don't know. It was different then. Sometimes, I'm not even sure I was actually there. I'd come back to the States, and everything was normal, as if there were no war going on. I don't even know if what I remember is what really happened. We'd better go now. It's getting late," he said, standing up.

I looked around the office and it, too, seemed to shrink with Dad's fading memories.

He took the stack of journals and turned off the lights, locked the door. I watched him walk down the hallway to the elevator. As he was walking, he took out one of the journals, folded it open and began reading again. I pushed the elevator button for him, but he didn't notice when it arrived at our floor. The doors opened then closed shut.

"Did you find what you wanted?"

"No," he said, with a look of disappointment. "There's got to be something else."

"Sorry," I said.

For a minute, Dad looked lost, the way Hawkeye looked on *M*A*S*H* last night, and he reached over and gathered me up, held me to his chest.

"I'm sorry too, Lucy."

I remembered the episode clearly. It was about a wounded Korean woman who had been captured. An officer thought she might be a guerilla and wanted to question her, but Hawkeye wouldn't allow it.

He'd just wanted to heal her, make her better.

Lucy

ও

Clouds marked the sky like tire tracks when Dad drove me to my grandparents' Spanish bungalow on Kings Road. My grandfather, David, opened the wrought iron gate and came out to greet us. He walked out slowly, cautiously, as if he were a child trying not to slip out of his shoes. He had a short, graying beard and pool-blue eyes. Dad walked me to the door like he usually did, but this time he hesitated, and for a moment I thought he might come in with me.

"Why don't you stay with Lucy, Aaron?" David posed the question, once again, and I felt bad for my grandfather, sorry for the way he asked Dad to stay each time he dropped me off. He was like the old man down the street from us who'd go out to his mailbox hours after the mailman had come and gone, still hoping for a letter.

"I can't. I have work to do." Dad shook his head, without looking up at his father, and I hated the way Dad turned away from him.

David didn't protest and I was glad there was no argument this time. It was always on the doorstep that they quarreled, as though their one agreement was not to bring their disappointments into the house.

"Come in Lucy," Ruth suddenly appeared at the door and she hurried me inside. Skilled in suffering, Ruth was an expert in overseeing every slight, imagined or real, getting it over with dispatch.

"Let him go, he's got work to do," she said, pulling at David's elbow. "He has a lot on his mind."

My grandmother knew how to gauge my father's moods, like a carpenter with a level, she eyed him for every misalignment. Ruth was stout and short, and looked nothing like her photograph in the den. It was Ruth as a thirteen-year-old in a spotted dress, trimmed in lace, a girl with faint smile, a girl who'd dreamed of being an architect. Behind her, the outlines of a window, only a hint of light.

My grandfather closed the door and I could hear the gate wince shut, then Dad's car driving off. David hugged me and I came into the living room. I liked their house, the line of the roof tiles, their terra cotta color, and the stained glass window overlooking the small front lawn.

Like Dad, David also had a desk, but it was in the corner of the living room. There were no locks and on top of the desk he kept a messy jumble of things—black and white chessmen, and silver dollars, which he stored in empty, yellowed medicine bottles topped with cotton balls. There were also copies of the *Daily Forward* in Yiddish, and a letter he'd started to write to a friend, his handwriting rising and falling like a heartbeat. A worn first aid kit hung from a strap over the back of the wooden desk chair. It overflowed with bandages and bottles of rubbing alcohol.

"What's that?" I asked.

"Before we came to this country, I wanted to study medicine," he said with a sigh.

"Hitler took care of that," Ruth interjected.

"We were lucky. At least we got out in time, and our Aaron had the opportunity to be a doctor, " David continued.

Dad was only four when my grandparents left Eastern Europe in 1937, David had once told me, just a year before Hitler invaded Austria.

"Did you bring your homework with you?" Ruth asked me.

"I forgot."

She shook her head. "Never have idle hands, Lucy. Did you eat?"

Ruth didn't greet me with a kiss. Cooking and baking was her way of serving affection, and she got up every morning at six to cook and do battle with the pots and pans, her powder-blue apron secured by two safety-pins on her housecoat like war medals. I followed Ruth into the kitchen. The table was covered with powder, and Ruth began separating the egg yolks from the whites into wells of flour. A tin of bittersweet cocoa powder was open nearby, a trail of cocoa spilling onto the table. Once a month, Ruth would bake dozens of hard sugar cookies, the oven ablaze with heat.

I stood and watched her. When she wasn't cooking, Ruth would sometimes sit at the kitchen table and draw sketches of the buildings she imagined. On the table was the yellow, Stanley tape measure she usually kept in her pocket. Often she'd pull out the metal strip from its holder, catch the end on something and measure a room, or sometimes, the outside of the house. She'd write the measurements down on a small notepad and a tiny pencil she sharpened with a knife. She'd measure once, then again, not trusting her results, as though each computation was vital, her calculations some kind of containment, a fort against the outside world.

Ruth undid the safety pins and took off her apron, then hung it up on a nail in the pantry.

I walked over to the dining room. The china cabinet had glass doors with a little key. The cabinet itself was filled with silver—old wine cups and candlesticks, a menorah. Every Friday morning, my grandmother took each piece out of the cabinet and put them on an old tablecloth on top of the dining table. She also took out the silver polish, chalky-pink. I'd seen the rare look of contentment on her face as she rubbed the silver with a soft polishing cloth, brightening the darkened crevices.

My mother used to do it this way, she'd said, closing her eyes. I'd known she was thinking of the other photos in the family room, her mother and sisters, the girls with bows in their hairs against a velvet curtain, leaning dainty against a Roman column. They'd stayed behind in Europe. Sent to a slave labor camp, they'd all disappeared without a trace.

I followed my grandfather into the kitchen where he scooped up a handful of salted peanuts from a brown paper bag in the pantry. The pantry was full of twine and string retrieved into balls, plastic knives and forks, washed and reused, bent nails, straightened, stored in baby food jars.

"What's all this?" I asked about her stockpile.

"It could be of use, someday, you never know," Ruth said. Was her stash some insurance policy for some desperate times ahead? "We never threw anything out, *then*, when I was growing up," the word "then" flung out into the air like a punctuation mark.

David went to the living room and spilled the peanuts on the coffee table. He settled down into the couch and began shelling the nuts, cracking them open one by one.

"Sit down next to me," he said, patting down the sofa pillow, and I joined him there.

"Don't say a thing now," David warned Ruth who was standing in the doorway of the kitchen. "Not a word."

"When is he going to come and talk to us about going back there?"

"Not now," David pleaded with her.

"The past always catches up with you," she continued, and her words seemed to eat away at her, like rust on metal. "There's no escape."

"Ruth, stop it." My grandfather was adamant now.

"Aaron doesn't look well," Ruth's voice suddenly melted with my father's name.

"You look tired, Lucy," David said, ignoring her.

"I'm fine."

"You want to take a nap here on the sofa?"

I shook my head.

My grandfather smelled good, like tea. I loved his stories, his big hands, the veins bulging from the work he did in the garden, the trace of dirt under his fingernails. David knew everything about the garden. He'd take me to all the nurseries; the small ones crammed with pots and plants, narrow pathways under arbors bursting with climbing vines, and the commercial ones in the north valley, with acres of plants in attentive rows, like planes waiting to take off. David said he could tell the difference between the trees by the sounds they made; the flapping fronds of the palms, the whistle of lacy birches and willows. He said the oaks were the only trees that shuddered, like people. He understood the geography of the mountains and canyons, knew exactly where the first rains of the season cut a path. He'd take me there sometimes, and we'd wait at the exact spot where the first trickle appeared, then made its way down the mountainside, finding its strength, spilling into a torrent.

"I can tell you about Joseph again, the time he was in prison and he interpreted Pharaoh's dreams. Aaron used to like that story."

"Not today."

I might have been able to fall asleep with him and his stories, outside, on a bench in the garden, like I sometimes did, but I couldn't do it here, in Ruth's living room. "She's fine," Ruth said. "She doesn't need a nap."

David handed me some peanuts.

"It's all Hitler's fault," Ruth sputtered from the kitchen. "*Yemach shemo*," she cursed, flinging a dishtowel to the floor.

I'd heard it often. It meant "may his name be erased," and there was no more potent curse, nothing worse for Ruth than the obliteration of a name.

It was because of the others, her parents and younger sisters, and all the ones who never had their names uttered again.

"A name is important. Remember that, Lucy."

"A name is important," I repeated, and for some reason I thought of the stack of books I used to flatten my photographs while they were drying. I could feel the weight of them.

"Don't forget, Lucy."

It was Ruth's burden—the ones who were exterminated— but they were my burden too, and Dad's.

Mai

The water was everywhere, all around us. I'd never seen so much, an outrage of water, filling in the horizon, mocking me. I was thirsty but we were only allowed one cup each day from the water that was stored in small, plastic containers on the deck. Linh and Thanh pressed close to me at the back of the fishing boat and there was no room to move. Streaked with rust, the wooden planks were splintered, raw beneath me. I didn't hear the sound of the engine anymore, just the water. It, too, licked thirstily, lapped up at the boat. There were too many people for the small boat and it sat low, beneath the waterline.

Van had been right when he'd warned us that the trip would be dangerous, but Linh and Thanh had both insisted on leaving, each for their own purposes, and no one had asked what I wanted.

I knew we should have never left Vietnam, its clay-red earth, muddy waters. I closed my eyes to remember the pastel light, the feel of water in the sky, the mist and clouds gathering, hovering like gauze over mountains.

The shutters had kept out the heat of the afternoon, but not the sounds of the caged birds in the market. There, the sky had been my opium, my sleep narcotic.

Now it was gone and I could hardly sleep.

We'd left Van's apartment in the dark of night. Thanh woke me up and made me wear three shirts. We all got into a small truck that was waiting. Along the way, the truck stopped to pick up four other people I'd never seen before. After riding for about an hour, we arrived at a small town. We walked in the dark until we came to a house where we hid in a back room. Hours later, a man came and brought us to the bank of a river. At the river's edge, Thanh picked up a handful of wet dirt and spread it on my face. Before dawn, a small sampan took us down the river.

Everyone had been quiet on the river, but I could hear people move around, like snakes in a bush. When we saw a signal light, a larger fishing boat picked us up and we headed out to the open sea.

The first morning on the boat, the seawater had been light blue. Later, the water turned blue-black. We passed the float marking international waters, a bright yellow buoy against the ocean.

At night there had been no light, but a deadly quiet, only the sound of someone praying, and on the other end of the boat, a woman gave birth to a child. I could hear the mother's labor pains, her weeping, but I never heard the baby cry.

"A stillborn," a woman's voice had whispered, and something fell into the black water, the sound of it so small, so tiny, even the waters took pity on the child that never took a breath.

In the morning, Thanh began to dole out the food she'd brought along in a cloth bag to Linh and me.

"Our food is running out," she said, and wrapped the bag tighter around her waist.

"Give my portion to Mai," Linh said, pushing Thanh's open hand away. "I'm not hungry."

On the third day, the seawater turned purple. Both Linh and I lost our *nons* before we'd boarded—and had no defense against the sun. I felt the heat against my head and I wanted to swim out to the dolphins and whales that followed us. I stood up, the sun drilling a hole through me, and I climbed onto the side of the boat. I wanted

66

to find them, touch their slippery gray coats just beneath the water. Someone caught my arm just as I fell.

"Let me go," I cried out.

"No."

It was Linh, and I pounded my fist into her when she pulled me down beside her and yanked me to her breast. I could feel her heart pounding in her chest, how it raced in her throat. I punched her again, but she said nothing, just kept her grip on me, tight. Her hand became twisted and coiled, a rope against my wrist, and she wouldn't let go.

"Leave me."

Leave me to the water, to its coolness.

"I need you, Mai. I love you."

"No, you don't."

You don't love me.

I stopped fighting her, submitted to her will, but I knew she only loved the part of me that was him, her American. She'd only clung to me because I would be her offering to him, her barter when she found him. He didn't want her anymore, but maybe he still wanted me.

At night, when the stars came out, I punished her for that. I dove in, swam into her sleep, slid inside of it. Before, she'd let me in, let me have her sleep, her dreams, parceling them out easily for me, one at a time, like little gifts. But now, on the boat, she wanted to keep her dreams for herself and she fought me over them, struggled against me. But I was stronger than Linh and I wrestled with her spirit, prying them away from her.

※

They take the train that follows the winding mountain tracks to the highlands, to Da Lat. The American can arrange for a helicopter, but Linh wants to take the train, close her eyes in the long tunnels that suddenly appear, plunging them into pitch black. She wants to hear the train hissing and creaking on rail ties toward the denseness of the forest.

From the train, she can see the water. Grandfather's summer villa sits among the lofty pine forests and watery lakes. High above the coast, the mountain air is cool, dry, away from the monotonous pull, the sticky wetness of the sea. Xuan Huong Lake rises from the mountains, like a shattered mirror, and it captures the sky, brings it down to the earth in pieces. There are other lakes, the Lake of Sighs, and the waterfalls, curtains of water that fall from clusters of rock. Orchids and poinsettias mass in the fields below.

When they reach the train station, three pointed roofs slice a muted sky. Under the central roof, a large clock sits atop the porte-cochere and two rows of columns.

Linh takes the American to the villa Grandfather had bought from a Frenchman, before they all abandoned their silk factories, their tea and mulberry plantations. She shows him the palace of the last Emperor, last of the Nguyen dynasty, Bao Dai. The emperor had a terrace just for watching the moon, and a well-tended garden of lilies and roses, avocadoes and guavas. He had the company of his beautiful concubine, but he wasn't content and he abandoned his palace on the hilltop. She shows the American this place because it is a place of desertion.

The American takes her dancing in a club and her cheeks redden. She can smell the Chanel on her own neck, the way it mixes with his sweat when she dances with him.

Further up the mountain, five volcanoes peak, watching over the raised thatched huts. The huts are built on stilts like the long-legged birds that fly over the mud-filled lagoons. They have dinner on the veranda of the villa, the sun setting like strips of mango. He takes out his camera and asks the houseboy to take a photograph of them leaning on the balcony. He puts his arm around her shoulder just as the boy takes the photo, and his hand is blurry with the motion, like a bird in flight.

For dessert, they eat strawberries grown in the fields of Da Lat while the houseboy refills the wineglasses. The American's promises fly across the night air like faint fireflies, spits of fire. Linh looks down at her wristwatch.

It has stopped.

She reaches over the table and spills the wine on the white linen tablecloth.

Don't promise.

She doesn't want to hear his words, any words. They can be altered, easily crossed out. The words are no more than witchcraft, mumbo jumbo, wily conjurers of false visions. His promises are opium, the poppy when the petals drop and the sap oozes. They are the small ball attached to a needle, toasted and twisted over a spirit lamp, the softness of the opium pellet inserted, the pipe inhaled.

Don't spoil the words.

They take Grandfather's bedroom for themselves, sleeping in the mahogany poster bed, carved high off the ground. They roll down the netting that clings, snags at each post.

He traces the carvings etched deep into the wood with his hands. He has beautiful hands, long hands and he runs his hands across her body slowly, like a healer. From the tip of her foot to the top of her head, he follows the curve of her hips, her landscape, the well of her neck. He hypnotizes her with his hands.

There is no fairness in the way he uses his hands.

And beyond their window is a night of monkeys, squealing in the woods.

Lucy

My grandfather drove me back home, and I walked around to the side door. Through the open window, I heard Mom speaking on the phone and I thought I might be able to sneak into the house, maybe even watch some TV without her knowing. She was often on the phone, talking with her girlfriend, Irene, from Studio City, or Debbie from across the street. She always seemed more animated on the telephone than when her girlfriends came by for lunch, more at ease, it seemed, when they were just voices, unseen, disconnected.

"Is that you, Lucy?" Mom called out like radar.

I heard the phone's receiver snap back into its cradle.

"It's me."

I grabbed the latest *TV Guide* off the table in the back hallway and walked through the living room to the kitchen. The study was my father's, but the rest of the house belonged to my mother. I walked past the fireplace, floating above the floor: a wall of lava rocks rising, rough, like the face of a mountain from behind. In the entrance were built-in planters of philodendron and drowsy fern. Close to the kitchen, I could already see the pebbly linoleum, the wallpaper, blinding with bright, yellow flowers. She'd just redecorated the kitchen last summer, and every other week she polished the honey-colored cabinets with Lemon Pledge and a soft, white rag.

"Sit down, Lucy. How about some hot chocolate? I'll have some too."

"All right."

I'd have to sit with her now, but at least I'd have a chance to check out the new *TV Guide*, see what was playing on *Three's Company* tonight.

"Come and knock on our door."

In the last episode, Jack and Chrissy were handcuffed together and Janet was jealous.

Maybe tonight I'd try out some color film when I took photographs of the show.

Mom watched me flip open the guide for a minute and looked me over, scanning me for clues. I smiled widely at her and she smiled back. Mom was easy to read. Like a Polaroid, she showed herself too quickly. It was harder to make her face go dark, but I also knew how to do that. I'd learned it from Dad, but I wasn't sure I always enjoyed this power I had, we both had, over her.

Maybe I'd have more to say to her if she'd get out of the house, and go to work.

"Diane's mom just got a great job," I said.

"I already have a job. I'm a doctor's wife," she replied, her stock answer.

She had a degree in social work from San Diego State, but had stopped working after I was born. She always talked about how she loved to ride horses, had even placed in some amateur races, but it was just talk—I'd never seen her ride. She didn't do anything, didn't even go to a shrink, like Diane's mother.

Mom was the reason Dad spent so much time away from the house. She was the problem.

"How about going to the group I told you about?" I continued, trying to push her buttons.

I was in a bad mood today, and bent on hitting as many sore spots as I could, all the possible points of contention. I'd been trying to get her to join one of those encounter groups where people sat on the floor and wrote down their dreams, but she'd always refused.

"Where did you go last night, Lucy?" she said, ignoring my question.

"To the movies," I said. I'd been over at Diane's house, but sometimes I lied to her for no reason. Just for the sake of lying.

After all, she lied too. As much as she was home, every once in a while, she'd disappear for a day, never telling us where she'd been. At first I'd thought her disappearances were manufactured—to worry Dad, and make us appreciate her more. But then I realized she vanished for her own reasons, a kind of test of her aloneness, whether she could be separate from us.

I knew how she felt, though—to be seduced and repulsed by a lie, being its recipient, by wanting to know, not wanting to know.

I sat down at the kitchen table while Mom opened one of the cabinets and took out the Nesquik.

"Lucy?" she started, then changed her mind.

It had been my mother's idea to name me Lucy, but I'd always wished she'd named me something else.

A name was important.

Why couldn't she have named me Kelly, like the girl from *Charlie's Angels*?

Good Morning, Angels.

Good Morning, Charlie.

I looked up at her as she reached up to the top shelf to get the cocoa tin. She'd put her hair back in a ponytail and was wearing knee-high boots. She looked great in boots.

I could see why Dad was attracted to her, and she too would rush down the stairs whenever she heard him at the door. I could see the chemistry between them, the way they were both drawn to beauty, he to the way she simplified it for him, she, to beauty's complications. It was the one thing Mom was clever at—being beautiful. She knew how to get things from Dad, the kidney-shaped pool he added to our house, the silver Toyota he bought her for her birthday, but she didn't care for any of it. They were only some kind of payback for her, some strange evidence he still wanted to please her.

Mom turned around and glanced out of the kitchen window that overlooked the backyard.

"There are no oranges this year," she said, puzzled, as if the missing oranges were a bad sign, as though some important life cycle had been disturbed, and she was right. Every October, the orange tree was full of fruit, but there were none this year. "Dad took you out to his office this morning?" Mom turned away from the window and put the water kettle on the stove.

"Just to the office."

"Did your father tell you about his trip? He's going to be away for a few weeks."

Your father.

The way she pronounced it, the word "father" sounded like someone falling off a cliff. She started it off high and ended low, muffled at the end, as though she'd turned down the volume.

"I guess so…"

She wanted to know more, but Mom only knew how to slide around a subject, come up to it from behind. She could be crafty, but I too had learned how to negotiate minefields. I'd learned that from her.

Instead of the coffee mugs we normally used in the kitchen, Mom spooned out heaping teaspoons of instant cocoa into her best porcelain cups. She was being unusually rough with them, as though daring them to break. I knew she was waiting for me to say more. When I didn't, she continued. "I see you've left your nails alone since we went to the nail salon together," Mom observed. "They're looking better." she almost hummed. "I'll have to take you back there and we can both get manicures next time around."

"That place had nothing to do with me stopping to bite my nails."

I stuffed my hands into my pockets. I didn't want her cocoa. When Dad and I were alone, he'd make me coffee.

Dad liked it black and strong—to get him through the nights.

Mom looked at me closely

"You look tired," she said. "Maybe you should rest before dinner."

"I'm fine."

Wasn't that what Ruth had said? I was fine.

"But you've got dark circles under your eyes," she said, biting her lip.

"I'm like Dad. I don't need a lot of sleep," I said, reopening the *TV Guide*.

"I guess you are," she said, narrowing her eyes, searching for some part of herself in me. She was almost squinting, like I did, when I tried to make out an image buried in shadows of a negative.

"Just like Dad," I repeated, hopeful she wouldn't find any fragment, any piece of herself.

Then her lips cracked a smile and I knew I'd been beaten. She'd found what she'd been looking for, she'd met herself in me.

Could I be like her?

"I suppose it's because of all those nights in the hospital, at the lab," she went on, as she poured the steaming hot water from the kettle into the cups.

Mom's voice trailed off. Dad wasn't the only one whose sleep was interrupted. Those sleepless nights belonged to Dad, but they belonged to her too, to me.

Like last night. I was having a strange dream that I'd been walking for days. When I reached the top of one hill, there was another, and my legs became heavy. I started slowing down and I couldn't walk anymore. But then, everything flipped around, a page turned, shifting, and I wasn't on the ground. The hills had given way, and everything was flat, watery, mutating into an ocean. There were dots everywhere, grids of intersecting lines, popping with electricity against each other, as if I'd come too close to a television screen. Then I moved back, saw the outlines of boats. I tasted the salt.

The phone woke me up. I'd heard Dad's voice answering it.

"I'll be right over," I'd heard him say.

He'd gotten up, but he didn't turn on any lights. He was used to finding his clothes in the dark and he dressed quickly, silently.

I'd heard his car back out of the driveway.

Mom had stayed in bed, but she couldn't fall back to sleep, so she turned on the TV. Then she got up and slipped on her robe, walked over to the window and opened it. It was her sleepless night too. I knew because I'd peeked into her bedroom, and checked on her, made sure she was all right.

Don't worry, I'd whispered. He'll be back.

He always comes back to us.

Mai

I t was the smallest speck, a dot on the horizon. I didn't believe Thanh when she said it was land. She'd lied to me before—in Saigon, when she'd said she had no money for food, and all that time, she'd kept her precious rings, her gold hidden between her breasts. It was her rings that had bought us passage on the boat, the jade ones she'd dug up one night in the garden of the old villa and kept to herself.

After four days, everyone was sick from the sea, the smells on the boat, everyone except Thanh. The days out on the water seemed to have made my grandmother stronger, even more determined. She was already planning, figuring, where we would go, how we would get there. I saw the calculations written on her forehead, her merchant thoughts.

Slowly I noticed that the dot grew. There were signs of land, birds hovering, and garbage floating by. The people at the front of the boat yelled excitedly and everyone stood up. Soon after, a ship came by and guided our boat into a port.

We landed on Galang, one of the Anambas Islands of Indonesia. The people from the Red Cross greeted us when we got to shore and showed us the showers, gave us clean, used clothing. I found a white shirt in a pile of clothes and I took it for myself, because white was a color of doctors, not refugees. The other children immediately wanted to stretch their legs and play, but I only wanted to eat the coconuts I found near the water, and suck out their salty milk.

The refugee camp on Galang was called Kuku, they told us and Thanh ran ahead of the others to the barracks, finding three beds for us near the corner.

"It's the best spot," she announced. "Between two walls." She was proud she'd pushed someone else out of the way to get that space. But it didn't look like the best spot to me. It looked like the rest of the shabby room.

In the morning, the Red Cross gave us tickets for food—a bag of rice, beans, and two cans of meat. I walked around the camp to orient myself. There were makeshift streets, stalls where refugees set up small businesses. There was a bakery, a man who sold salt by evaporating seawater, even a jeweler. The camp was a good place for Thanh. She soon learned how to trade part of our Red Cross portions with the locals for dry squid and fish.

One day, I stole cigarettes from a boy in the barracks next to us. I crept right up to him when he was asleep, and grabbed them from him, but Linh saw me smoking out in the back of our quarters, and took the cigarettes away from me. She dragged me by my shirt collar inside, where Thanh was counting money.

"They're bad for you," she said, but instead of throwing them away, she put the box under her pillow.

"Let her have them," Thanh spoke up. "She can sell them."

"No," Linh said. "I am her moth—"

I thought she would say mother, but she stopped. Even Linh understood she'd given up her claim to the word.

I knew why she'd taken them from me. They were American cigarettes, Marlboros, the kind Linh's American used to smoke. She'd wanted them for herself, to smell, inhale. She hadn't seen a pack of Marlboros since he'd left Saigon, and she thought she was closer to him, now that we were on this island, now that she had the odor of his cigarettes on her hair again.

I didn't really want the cigarettes anyway. It was the box I wanted, the red and white top with the long, black writing, stretched out, like her tall American. I liked to flip it open and shut. It was an ideal place for the little things I'd pick up, other people's throwaways. For a moment, I imagined myself in there too, small, like a seashell in a dark chamber, where no one would find me.

I saw the way the men eyed Linh in the camp. But she would have nothing to do with them, wouldn't even look in their direction. Sometimes, they looked at me too, and I followed Linh's example, never found their eyes. The other women in the camp were jealous of Linh, envious of her beauty, but Linh never noticed. They didn't see she was as empty as the cigarette box I'd found.

She still had the torn-up dictionary I'd given her in Ho Chi Minh City. She pulled it out from under her mattress and opened it.

"You see the punctuation marks? There are no punctuation marks in Chinese. But in English, there's the apostrophe. It shows belonging, Mai. And the parentheses, they are curved to enclose."

"I'm busy now." I was tired of her short moments of lucidity. They were only a ruse that left me craving more.

Linh sat down on the makeshift bed, her eyes open, but after a while I realized she wasn't awake. She was trying to trick me now, dreaming her dreams, conjuring her memories by day, so I wouldn't snatch them away. But I was as cagey as Thanh and understood what she was doing, and I crawled beneath Linh's cot, became her shadow, by night and by day.

※

The American is tired.

He's seen too much. He's sewn them up, their flesh, bloodied, boys, bodies torn apart by shrapnel, the mines. At the Third Field Hospital, the doctors tend the VIPs. But he goes out on his own time to the bases, to Da Nang and Cam Ranh Bay, to the evacuation hospitals, working triage. He flies in the choppers to the jungles, the countryside of bomb craters, and shell casings, the villages leveled like matchsticks by sticky, burning napalm.

I don't want a son. I will never have a son, he tells Linh.

They are having drinks at the Duc bar and he orders her a Bloody Mary. I want only girls, he says. At first, she thinks it is because of the war, because of all the young men the war has taken.

Then she realizes it is something else.

He is a man who lives with men, who fights alongside them, but at home he surrounds himself with women.

He has a girl, he says and then shows her a photograph. Linh steadies herself against the edge of the bar and holds the photograph in her hand. She closes her eyes and sears it into her memory, etches it there. It is important for her to know her, the little girl with wisps of bangs, the green eyes, like her father. It is important to remember the little girl, to pass on the memory of her.

He is quiet, too quiet. He doesn't talk like the rest of them, the others. He doesn't use too many words, like the other Americans she's met before. She appreciates the sparseness of his words.

He is not like the others, the ones who use words like bath water, to wash, rid themselves of what they see, what they do. They have a new lexicon of combat, a shorthand of bastardized words, acronyms, arbitrary combinations of letters, as if Vietnam must be cut up to be understood.

We're heading out to China Beach for R&R.

We clobbered that VC unit back there, didn't we?

LZ, LBJ, DMZ, AWOL.

Worse, they revel in their pidgin Vietnamese, looting words like war trophies.

That papa san is dinky dau.

The words can unify and they can separate; they can bring people closer together, and tear them apart.

She met another American at the Duc bar once.

I'm a tunnel rat, he said.

His eyes were yellow with jaundice. He was one of those who volunteered to clear the underground tunnels, to flush out VC from the miles of tunnels. He was down there, in the cities underground. He saw their special ventilation ducts and shafts, the wells, hospitals below ground. He saw the booby traps and bats, scorpions. Those damn gooks were waiting around the next dark turn.

Show me the tunnels, she told him.

You're crazy.
I want to see them.

The others talk and talk, can't stop talking, sometimes slow on their stashes of marijuana, other times, fast. They talk about the protesters at home, the draft dodgers, the peaceniks and the hippies, the sit-ins at Berkeley.
They don't know shit.
They ramble on about Johnson and Nixon. They buy hairspray and lipstick at the PX in Cho Lon for the bar girls they meet.
Hey, I just don't want to go home in a Glad bag.
But he is quiet, almost as if speech is an impediment, a flaw, and he never talks about going home.
Linh likes his wordlessness, his silence, even when it rips them both apart. He is like the quiet before the Tet fireworks lit up the sky. He is the coil of their red firecrackers, filled and brushed with silvery gunpowder, ready to explode.
It is his hands that speak for him, the way they shake and tremble sometimes, when he holds the drink in his hand at the bar, his fingerprints all over the tall glass. His hands say everything about him, say more than any of his words.
Linh looks at the photograph one more time, and then gives it back to him.
The girl looks like her father, like him.

Mai

Kuku had a small clinic and I'd find all kinds of excuses
to walk by there. Near the water, the clinic took in its light and it was
always crowded with people, some on litters, others in wheelchairs.
There were children with open wounds, old men with scars, holes
where bullets had entered and exited their bodies. They'd always
come out with something in their hands—bandages or little bottles
of tablets. I liked to hear the visiting doctors talk to each other in
English and French.

"The patient is dehydrated," one doctor called out too loud, as
though he were still in a large hospital. He'd forgotten he was only
in a small clinic, where his voice didn't have to carry.

Their words were fascinating, long, sometimes widening into
four syllables. Maybe that was the reason Linh fell in love with her
American, for his words, the special terminology of medicine, words
born of Latin and Greek. Or did she fall in love with him because
he understood what it was to have a daughter?

Linh was a fool. He wouldn't come for us if he already had
another daughter.

What was she like, this other daughter? A better daughter than me, I was sure.

The doctors complained about not having enough supplies or good equipment. I listened closely to them as they spoke. I strained to hear their names. I came to see their white doctor coats, to find him, his traces, Linh's American.

Once, I stood too close to the door and someone in white pulled me aside.

"What are you doing here?"

I didn't answer.

"The clinic's off limits unless you're sick."

I was sick, ill with the thought of him, and I ran off, but I came back because I couldn't take even the smallest chance that I'd miss finding him for Linh.

Thanh warned me to stay away from the clinic, but I didn't obey her. I knew she was afraid, worried I might actually find him. Thanh knew if he came back, she'd lose her hold over Linh.

Linh wouldn't walk past the clinic, but she found reasons to send me there.

"I need an ointment for my leg, Mai," she said, one late afternoon after a long rain, and I went to get it for her. The sky was still wet with clouds and a perfect breeze fanned the island.

No one chased me away this time, and a new French nurse gave me two small oranges along with the ointment in a sack. I brought the fruits back to Linh, already impatient for my return. She sniffed around me, as if I'd taken on the clinic's scent, its alcohol and disinfectant, the shiny instruments, dark vials and syringes. She made me sit down on the cot, and inspected my hands, checked my pockets, as if I were hiding contraband, evidence of him. She ate one of the oranges, and put the other away, then went to bed.

Soon after midnight, a soft light bathed the barracks cots. Linh arose and I followed her to the clinic where she sat beneath one of the windows, listening to the sounds inside. They were tiny sounds, but her hearing was as good as mine and I could see she took them in, like oxygen. She took in the sounds of hospital beds, their squeak on the floor, the pouches of IVs, dripping, deflating. She fell asleep with the sounds of the nurses, their quiet chatter in the dispensary.

She looked so pretty, asleep in the moonlight, her hair falling to the ground. She was a plume, and I knew how Linh's American had fallen in love with her.

I looked up at the full moon against the night sky. If everything fell with the pull of gravity, why didn't the moon fall too? Why didn't it drop out of the heavens, and land in Linh's hands?

I crawled over to where Linh slept.

"You're close," she said, stirring, talking to her American, and the closer she thought we were getting to him, the longer her dreams became, taking over. For Linh, the reflection of her life was becoming truer than its image.

"It's from the Sanskrit," Linh said, half-asleep, the fragrance of orange peel and rain on her fingertips.

"What is?" I asked.

"Orange. It comes from the phrase *naga ranga*. It means 'fatal for elephants'."

"Yes, Linh," I said although I saw she fell back asleep.

There was a history, a story, in this simple word. Somewhere in ancient India, it had been born of a remark and it had crept over borders, insinuating itself, oozing into other worlds. Language didn't stand immobile. Like a caravan, it crossed the artificial demarcations, geographies of maps. English was full of borrowed words; the Malay's bamboo and rattan, the Spaniard's armada, the Persian's bazaar and divan, Linh said, and it comforted me to think I wasn't a thief, but also a borrower, a guardian of her memories. Maybe I hadn't tossed her dreams away all this time, out into the darkness as I'd thought.

Maybe I'd sent them on a journey, to the other daughter.

※

The Mekong River flows into the sea. Starting in the Himalayas, it cuts through China, then through Burma, Laos, and Cambodia, until it reaches Vietnam, where it splits into nine estuaries, ending in the South China Sea. Called Cuu Long, the nine dragons, it separates into hundreds of veins of water, mazes of canals, and it is as if the land has surrendered itself to the sea, allowed itself to be overtaken. But it is the water that brings life to the land, feeds the rice paddies and sugarcane, the fertile ponds of shrimp and fish.

The American wakes up in the middle of the night, bathed in sweat, the wet of the Mekong still on his back. Linh takes a damp cloth and wipes his face. He was in the delta that day, and he tells her about the bamboo and coconut, the nipa palms. It is where dikes once crisscrossed green, flooded fields that reflected the skies like giant mirrors.

Everything is different now. Even the land and plants, the insects and animals are the enemy. The reeds and the high water, the mangrove forests hide Charlie, its enemy guerilla bases. It is no longer the delta, but a zone, a parallel, the IV Corps Tactical Zone, home to the Ninth Infantry Division and Special Forces units. It is a place where the B-52s drop their bombs, napalm, oceans of fire, where the C-123 cargo planes spray defoliants, searing and charring the land to flush out the VC.

That morning he takes a MEDEVAC chopper deep inside in-country. When they land, the forests of fronds and bamboo are dense, cutting off his air. In the jungle, the only sounds are shrill, high up in the trees, or low on the ground. But he can hear it, he can feel the jungle breathing. There, he meets a kid from Indiana, another from Detroit, infantry grunts. They tell him their stories, and he gathers them like a farmer taking in sheaths of rice. They talk about the mama sans and the hooches, the Zippo raids and sweeps, the souvenirs they've swiped off their first kills. And when night falls, it is red, the sky bloodied.

What are we doing in this ugly-ass war?

They're just kids.

He's been inside the MACV headquarters on Pasteur Street, but they have never set foot in the Joint General Staff headquarters near Tan Son Nhut Airport. They've never been invited to Westmoreland's place in Saigon with the white trim and green shutters, a black Chrysler Imperial parked within the walled grounds. But they know his orders, the orders that tell them to move.

Keep moving.

Search and destroy.

The place is crawling with gooks.

They patrol, hack their way through, humping the boonies even after their buddies have caught a piece of shrapnel or are KIA *from mines and grenades, sharpened bamboo pungi stakes in camouflaged pits. What is the point of capturing a mountain ridge, only to have the* VC *return there the next day? Why blow up a bridge when Charlie rebuilds it overnight?*

We got two men down, Doc.

Sometimes I think my legs won't hold me, Doc.

I can't stop hearing it. I can't stop hearing the screaming when he got blown out of a hole, Doc.

Fire in the hole.

Cover me.

In a day, he knows them all. He knows who is a pothead, high on weed, who is on their second tour, who is a replacement. He knows them. They're called FNG*'s, the fuckin' new guys, the cherries. Bitching and griping, they still carry their packs heavy with shaving cream and combs, clean socks; they still kiss their* M-16*s. They'll learn soon enough to abandon all that crap when they are waist deep in water.*

He knows the officers. Some of them are only there to punch their tickets with a tour of combat duty. They'll get their fragging soon enough.

He is going back to Saigon, but doesn't want to leave them, doesn't want to leave the kid from Detroit, even though the mortar rounds are pounding, even though he is praying with them.

God. Just get me out of here, get me out of this lousy hellhole.

Please. Don't let me get hit.

But more than dying, he is afraid of surviving.

He knows the weight of that, of surviving, of those left to sweep up what is left behind when war is done.

It is night, when it all comes back to him, and his head is full of nightmares. She hates the word nightmare. It is unfair, derived from a night of old hags. Why must the nightmares be female demons, why must they be of women? His cries are like mournful trill, and Linh listens, tries to hold him close but he can't stand the touch of her, her smell. He can't abide Linh's clean sheets and pillows, throws them to the floor. She thinks of all of his words, the terminology of warfare, mutilated, mangled, turned inside out without hope for finding their spark; though for her the words are still alive. They are chameleons of time and place, thieves, borrowing from other languages, invented and blended, inherited, and they are hers. They still belong to her.

Linh doesn't say a word. She makes him tea, adding lotus flower and fragrant jasmine to the brew. She lies beside him on the bare bed, silent, so that the stories pass, flowing like water out to the sea.

Lucy

ᘐ

Dad was talking on the phone in his study when I came home from school.

"Dad?"

"Can't talk now, Lucy."

He shut the bottom drawer of his desk. He'd been trying to get a special visa and in the last few days there had been long distance calls to offices in Washington D.C. and Sacramento, to people who could help him in New York.

On the desk was the registered letter he'd been waiting for all week. In the right-hand corner of the letter was a clutter of stamps and stained postmarks. Dad ripped open the envelope, reading the letter twice. Afterward, he put it down and went to the little bar in the corner of the room and made himself a Scotch and water. He took the glass with him upstairs to his bedroom and I followed him there.

His beat-up Samsonite was already on the bed.

I watched him open the top drawer of his dresser. Mom usually did the packing for him, but not this time.

He flopped the suitcase open and moved back and forth from

the closet to the bed, then to his tall dresser. On top of the dresser sat an opened pack of Marlboros.

"Are you smoking again, Dad?" I asked.

"No, just an old habit when I travel, I guess."

He folded and refolded his shirts on the bed, then changed his mind, returned some things back to the drawers.

"I won't need that. The less I take the better," he mumbled to himself, as if need was a dirty word.

I went downstairs, to see where Mom was. She was sitting at the kitchen table.

"He's chasing a ghost," she said to herself.

She stirred something in a mug. It was dark and I couldn't tell whether it was tea or coffee, and the kitchen seemed out of focus and grainy. Mom slowly brought the mug up to her lips with two hands, like she was praying. She'd left the spoon in the cup, but she didn't notice that it pressed hard against her cheek. I couldn't stand it anymore and I went to the den and turned on the TV. *The Facts of Life* was on.

"You take the good, you take the bad.

"You take them both and there you have, the Facts of Life."

How would it be to go away to a boarding school, like Blair and Tootie, Natalie and Jo? Maybe I could wear a blue blazer with a gold school crest, a blue tie and white shirt, and Mrs. Garrett could take care of me too. Maybe it wouldn't be so bad being away from them, not having a mother and father.

Mom and Dad both went to bed early, but I hardly slept at all. It was the moon that kept me awake. It was a full moon, and it streamed in through the window, past the blinds, leaving its watery stripes of light on my bed. I could feel it pulling me, and when I did finally sleep, it made my head full too, full of dreams. But they were only parts of dreams, slivers, like television programs interrupted, their signals all messed up.

Please stand by.

Do not adjust your set.

I was swimming in our pool, but it was different—long and

green, thick, the top covered with moss. I tried to hold on to it, but I felt myself sinking and I looked for the pool's edge, but at once it became an ocean and there was none. There was someone pulling me out, lifting me out from behind, but I couldn't see the person's face, and I only felt the strength in her hands. Dolphins swam alongside me, gray and bottle nosed, smoother than the water. All I could see were boats, hundreds of boats, and inside, a throng of people, the weight of them, tipping the boats over, and the image stayed with me.

Don't be afraid.

It's just a dream, but I tasted the green of the water.

Suddenly, I was with Dad and we were in a parking lot, looking for his car. We went from row to row, but he couldn't find it. Finally, the car appeared in the very last row, but Dad couldn't get it open. It was locked and he'd lost his key.

How did I get here?

In the morning, I watched Dad as he stood in front of his dresser mirror, struggling with his tie. He loosened it and refastened it three times.

"*Chaō, tam biet, cam on, ba,*" he practiced.

The words rolled around, formed in a different part of his mouth.

"What does *ba* mean?" I asked him.

"Father. It means father."

Finally, he just gave up and took the tie off.

Mom usually fixed his ties for him too. I'd seen her stand and face him, wind one end expertly into the other, tie a thin knot at the collar. Then finished, she'd smooth it down the length of his shirt and give him a kiss on the lips. But she didn't help him with his tie today. I looked out the window. She was outside on her knees, pulling up the flowers she'd carefully planted on the front lawn yesterday.

I pressed myself up against the windowpane as though it were a viewfinder, and saw a taxi pull up to the house and honk. It seemed almost out of focus to me and had the look of a green gum-wrapper, flattened and silvery beneath.

Dad came down the steps and set his bag down at the door for a moment. I followed him to the front door and there he held me for a long time, then he kissed me goodbye. I went back upstairs to the window and opened it, saw my mother still digging in the yard.

She stood up and he walked over to her, tried to kiss her.

"I have to go," I heard him say to her.

"You're only punishing yourself with all this," she said, turning away.

"Evelyn, you don't know what you're talking about."

Stop.

It was the first time I'd heard him call her "Evelyn" since the night I'd taken the car out without permission, and it didn't seem right for him to talk to her like that, to use her name as a snub.

He was in the taxi with the cab door shut when she yelled out at him.

"Can't you see what you're doing?"

It wasn't more than a minute, and the cab took off down the street. I looked hard at the place it had stood, and it was as if it had never been there. I wasn't even sure it had been green at all. Maybe it had been one of those yellow cabs or black. Maybe Dad hadn't left, or he was still inside, waiting for us to come in.

I stayed by the window for a while. It had been a morning of doors and windows—each was a frame, like photos in a three-dimensional family album, a diorama of comings and goings.

Mom was still in the flowerbed, crying, her knees sinking in the soft, upturned earth. Upstairs, the house felt as if it had no roof, nothing to contain it, and a wind ran through, taking me down the stairs. In the living room, an old photograph of Dad was on the mantle. I picked it up and read the inscription written on the bottom.

To Evelyn, my one love.

Then I put it back on the mantle. It was the same feeling I had in the darkroom when something was wrong with a photograph I'd printed, when I didn't want to hold it, not even by its edges.

I walked over to the study, to Dad's desk, and grabbed the handle of the bottom drawer. I yanked it hard, thinking it was still

Leora Krygier

locked, but it sprung open, and I fell backward with the momentum, the drawer falling to the floor.

It was empty, and I was certain Dad had taken whatever had been there with him, and for a moment I wanted to kick it aside. Instead, I put it back inside its opening in the desk and went up to my darkroom, slammed the door shut. I leafed through the contact prints I kept in a spiraled notebook and took one out. I brought the magnifying loupe to my eye. There was one shot I'd overlooked, the first on the roll I'd taken, a mistake when I'd loaded film in the kitchen the other day. I took out the corresponding negative strip to put on my light box and held the strip by the edges, felt the little notches in the film, the perforations that line the top and bottom and hooked into the mechanism that advanced the film. I sometimes kept the lens cap off when I loaded, and it was a photo of my parents, a half-frame only, their faces bleeding into darkness where the full light had partially hit the film, blackened it.

I knew exactly what I wanted to do and I mixed the chemicals, choosing a special paper, nubby, the kind used for watercolors. Then I calculated a short exposure time and set the clock. While I exposed the paper, I waved my hand between the lens and easel like a wand, softening their images, collecting them, and there they found the photograph's perfect image.

93

Lucy

I t was the Sunday after Dad left, and Ruth hummed to herself as she sat next to me on the Wilshire bus heading toward Santa Monica. The sounds were almost inaudible, a soft purring, but I was attuned to them. My grandmother always hummed when she got her own way.

It was the mid-afternoon, and an hour before she'd appeared on our front doorstep without warning. Ignoring the doorbell, she'd rapped on the door until Evelyn and I had both rushed to open it, then she announced she wanted to take me out to the palisades on the Westside. I looked at Mom, hoping she'd say something about Ruth not telephoning in advance, but my mother merely shrugged. We all knew my grandmother only showed up unannounced when she was worried about one of us, and Mom looked relieved that I, for once, seemed to be the object of Ruth's concern. I'd almost made a fuss, but then reconsidered. As much as I dreaded an outing alone with my grandmother, the thought of getting out of the landlocked valley, away from the house for a while, and heading out to the beach didn't seem so awful.

I took the aisle seat, Ruth the window. She was quiet for most of the long bus ride until we neared the border of Santa Monica. "You see the street names?" Ruth asked me. "Princeton, Harvard and Yale," she called out. "That's where your father should have studied. He was brilliant. He could have gone to any one of those schools, but he chose San Diego State. I told him it was a mistake to go to a state school, but he didn't listen to me," she said, holding her handbag securely on her lap. She was a tap, dripping old complaints.

"He did great in San Diego. He became a surgeon, didn't he?" I spoke up, annoyed she was forcing me to defend Dad just when I was mad at him for upsetting my mother, for leaving us.

"He could have been more. This sleep speciality, it's not really medicine. He shouldn't have given up surgery. He was doing something important, saving people's lives."

"Maybe he wanted a change."

"We don't always get to do what we want, Lucy. Sometimes, we have to do what is needed, what's expected of us. Our lives are not always our own. We sometimes live for others."

I steeled myself, waiting for the barrage, but suddenly she let her handbag drop to the floor. She turned away from me and opened the window. "I used to love the tram. I hardly get a chance to ride here in Los Angeles," Ruth said, a smile lighting her face.

For a moment, I could see her, the young girl who'd studied French and Latin in school, who had ridden the trolley in Iasi, in the Eastern half of Moldavia. She'd grown up there, in the city of "seven hillocks," known for its museums and poets. The stories she'd told me once about her childhood before the war, the walks through the gardens of Copou Park, the linden tree at its center, never seemed to apply to Ruth until I saw her here, the curve of the bus's interior arcing over her head.

We reached the last stop and got off the bus at Ocean Avenue. The air was cooler near the water, just a trace of salt, the sky bleached-white with a thin mist. At the end of Wilshire was the palisade, a swath of a park that stood two hundred feet on a bluff overlooking the water. Every year, erosion and heavy rains dissolved the sandy cliffs, reclaiming chunks of the park, fenced-off scant feet from the edge, and hurling rocks and soil down onto Pacific Coast Highway below. Somehow, though, the park endured and the possibility of collapse didn't deter the families who came to walk up and down the ribbon of green, the homeless who slept under the trees twisted by the sea winds.

"Isn't this wonderful, Lucy?" Ruth asked, and the gray-green Pacific in the distance deepened the sage of her eyes. I could see she felt at home here, where the light was so bright, it made shadows out of the people gazing out toward the ocean. Further on the sands, empty lifeguard stations dotted the coastline. Looking southward, everything was roundness and closure, from the planes taking off from the airport, circling into the sea and back, to the turn-of-the-century carousel pavilion on the old pier.

"Yes," I agreed.

"You're happy you came now," she said, and she took a deep breath, relieved at my concurrence.

I took in the air, and could feel it too. There was something about standing on the edge of a continent, the last few footprints of land melting into the ocean, and I saw Ruth come undone, like a bed slept-in, the tucked corners loosened away.

We walked, following the winding, palm-lined path, all the way to San Vicente Boulevard. The palm trees were stout at the beginning of the trail, becoming lithesome as we strolled to the north. We passed a group of elderly Russians playing chess, and again Ruth was transported to the geometry of the parks of her youth, their gravel and cobblestone.

"Where I came from, every public park was designed with special care, as if it was a building. People came every Sunday to walk. Here, in Los Angeles, people never walk. This is the only place where they do," Ruth declared, as we stopped to sit on a bench.

"Aaron used to love it here," she continued, and I knew this was where she came to forgive both the city and Dad for their transgressions. "We lived in one of those apartments across the street," Ruth said.

"I didn't know that."

"Yes, when we first came here to Los Angeles, we all stayed with my aunt who took us in the first year we were here. See the window on the second floor, there," she said pointing to the other side of the street. "It was a very small apartment, but you could see the ocean from the window. Every time I pass by it now, I can still imagine myself there. I can even see Aaron when he was little. Sometimes, I see my memories clearer than what I see today. Look," Ruth said suddenly, shaking her head.

On our side of the street, a couple waited for the light to change and cross. The man shook his finger at the woman, looking angry, but the woman ignored his rant and bent down to wipe the nose of her small child, standing nearby.

"You see, Lucy. We women are all lids. We cover up the boiling pots, swallow our own misery, don't we?"

"Yes," I answered her but the name on a building caught my eye. I'd read about the Camera Obscura facing the ocean. I hadn't realized it was here. There were only three like it in existence.

"Can we check it out before we go back?" I asked, pointing to the low building with a square tower.

"What's there?"

"I'll show you."

Ruth followed me up a flight of stairs. A wheel device that looked like a ship's steering wheel controlled the movement of a camera on the roof. A mirror was placed to reflect light through a convex lens, which displayed a picture on a large, white circular screen. I moved the metal turret, and we could see a one-mile radius from the pier in the south to Malibu in the north.

"It's amazing," my grandmother let out a little cry of excitement. Even Ruth was impressed by the panorama hidden away inside the dim room.

It was a living photograph.

"It's like when you poke a small hole and let light pass through a box in a dark room, the image on the opposite wall is upside down."

Ruth nodded with a look of understanding. "That's how I felt when we started to realize here what had really happened to the Jews during the war—like the world had turned upside down."

We stayed for a while, both circling around the image. On our way back to the Wilshire bus, Ruth stopped at a flower vendor and bought a large bouquet of orange roses wrapped in brown paper. She held the roses firmly in one hand and we walked back to our bus stop. Not far from the stop, I noticed a statue I hadn't seen when we'd arrived earlier.

"That's Santa Monica herself," Ruth explained, and we both looked up at the figure. "The city is named for her."

The saint stood there, like a compassionate touchstone between land and sea. She was dressed in a nun's habit—a pockmarked stone of beige. Her skirt fell down in folds, her nun's veil swirled to her waist in concentric half-circles. She didn't beckon with outstretched arms like other statues I'd seen but, rather, her hands were crossed over her chest, and Saint Monica's eyes were closed, as if she were asleep.

Ruth walked over and placed the bouquet delicately at the foot of the statue, then stepped away.

"What are you doing?" I asked.

The sound of my voice seemed to stir Ruth. "It's for your sake, Lucy," she said, "For you."

"What is?"

"I have to save your parents' marriage," Ruth answered, her mouth full of purpose. "I did it before. I saved it once…when you were little. I kept them together when there was a *probléme*," she said, digressing into French.

"What do you mean 'problem?' " I asked.

"Nothing. Nothing," she said, as if taking back a curse. "I told Aaron not to go there—to that Vietnam. I told him it was not for him, that he had other obligations—to carry on our name. I was the only one left of my entire family after the war, the only one, Lucy. Do you understand what it is to be the last?"

I understood it then—why Ruth had never forgiven Dad for volunteering to go to Vietnam, for putting himself in harm's way. He'd not only been the wellspring of all of Ruth's hopes, but also the cellar for all her demons—and he'd taken them along with him to Vietnam.

"Don't worry," she said, clear about her mandate to intercede.

I looked to the statue, and saw the beauty in her, what drew my grandmother to the figure against the curl of the ocean, but I was confused. Ruth was a woman who'd cheated Hitler out of another victim, and it didn't make sense to me that she wanted to pay homage to a pope's saint.

"You don't believe in saints."

"She's just a woman, like any other," she said, not admitting the contradiction. "Suffering is our religion," she said, leaning in closer to me, touching my chin. "Isn't it? And anyway, in the camp, in Transnistria, where they took my family to be their slaves, I know they prayed to all the gods, every single one of them."

There were tears in her eyes, but she brushed them away.

"We have to go back. Your mother is probably waiting for you and I don't want her to worry," Ruth said, looking at her watch.

The bus pulled up to the stop and we got on board. I looked out the rear window. Just beyond the saint, the western light began to yield to the earth's rotation, and it seemed like a signpost, a marker for the first leg of an odyssey. It, too, was intended for my sake—it blurred the faint demarcation between ocean and sky, smudging away the horizon.

Lucy

ॐ

Dad was only gone for a few days when I noticed my mother was different. It was the way she moved down the staircase, like ice dissolving into a puddle. It was also how she stood in the kitchen to make me breakfast, the way she took her time over the stove, the clothes and shoes she now tossed into the corners of every room like territorial markings, and I liked her better now that it was just the two of us in the house.

You're not in a hurry anymore, Mom.

ॐ

Alone with my mother, the days melted quickly. It was almost the end of fall, but the afternoons were still warm. The dry winds sometimes kicked up, and I was always thirsty, downing glasses of water from the fridge. Every few days, there'd be a phone call from Dad. His voice crackled, sounded far. There were other calls, and Mom would take a pad and pencil and write down the messages in her straight, neat, handwriting.

The weekend after he left, she drove us up the back roads to the marina in Ventura and we took a tour boat. There was barely a breeze that morning and the harbor was green, the color of glass. Out on the boat, the marina flattened to a thin strip as we made our way into deeper waters. We walked around the deck and Mom showed me the stern at the rear. We looked down at the water rushing up from beneath the ship's rudder.

"I thought you hated boats," I said to her.

"Who told you that?" she laughed, taking off her sunglasses. "Follow me," she said and we made our way to the front. Then she plucked a couple of wayward hairs off her sweater, releasing them over the water. "I've always loved the water."

The next Saturday, Mom put on a blue pantsuit and a silk scarf. We got into the car again and she turned into the onramp of the 101, heading downtown.

It was a chilly morning, and she turned the car heater on full blast, but she also rolled down all the windows, and the hot and cold felt right together. She got off near the Hollywood Bowl, taking Sunset Boulevard eastward. From a distance, I could see the Capitol Records building, round and tall, like old 45s stacked one on top of another, a needle rising from its top. Nearby was the Cinerama Dome, with its geodesic top. It was a honeycomb of concrete and I liked the curvature of the two buildings, the optimism of their roundness. When we got to Union Station, there were rows of palms at the entrance, the clock tower pressed up against the right side of the structure. Inside the station, there were high ceilings; a wide waiting room with oversized wooden chairs, linked together.

The train station felt like a church, with its Moorish tiles and arched windows, its flat chandeliers and marble floors and my mother looked as if she'd come to pray, to light a candle under the refuge of its wooden ceilings.

"We're going to Del Mar," Mom announced to the man behind the ticket window.

"What's there?" I asked, standing behind her.

"The race track." She took the tickets and waved them up in the air.

We followed the long, underground concourse to the train.

Florescent lights ran up and down the sides of the tunnel in edges of light, and I suddenly had a feeling of *déjà vu,* as if I'd been here before. Up a thin ramp and the light was blinding on the platform. I could smell the tracks and rail ties, and the white stones between. While we waited to board, I heard the sound of the train breathing, inhaling and exhaling on the track.

Later, our train took us along a ribbon of sand and ocean and I stood up and looked out the big window, saw the water in the distance, the dunes. I watched as a fog suddenly rolled in, swallowed the coastline, and turned the ocean water to milk. There was a rhythm to the train. It seemed to grab the rails beneath, tugging at them, like a pulse. Mom went to the dining car and she bought us large Cokes and two bags of Cheetos.

"This train goes all the way down to San Diego," she said. She was sipping her second Coke from a straw, her fingertips oily-orange. "I met your Dad on the train to San Diego.

"I didn't know you liked trains too." I looked at her. Someone had pulled down one of the back windows and her hair was flying up, framing her face.

"I used to," she smiled.

She looked content on the train and I didn't want to spoil it, but I couldn't help myself. I'd wanted to ask her for a long time. "Why didn't you have another child?" I asked.

"Your dad didn't want any more," she answered calmly, without hesitation.

"But what about you?" I persisted. I was sure it was Mom's fault I didn't have a brother or sister, that it was Mom who didn't want another kid.

"I'd always thought we'd have another baby, maybe another girl, like you Lucy, but your father didn't want to, not after 'Nam."

'Nam.

It should have been Dad who called it 'Nam. After all, he'd been there. But it was Mom who said it, chopped the word, Vietnam, in two. For Dad, it was a whole. For her it was a line in the sand, a before and an after.

We got off at the station in Del Mar, and Mom hailed a cab. When she told the driver we were going to the racetrack, he turned around and looked at her strangely.

"Racing season is over at that track."

"It doesn't matter. Drive there anyway," Mom said.

"Okay, lady," I heard him say under his breath.

Only a short ride to the racetrack, the road curved around like a sling. The driver stopped at the entrance and my mother gave him a big tip. I looked out to see two peach-colored, spiked towers standing above the empty parking lot. Mom spotted a security guard and walked over to talk with him. After a minute, she waved me over and he let us in.

Inside, Spanish fountains splashed water over enclosed patios that made a path to the track. Mom took out two sets of binoculars from her bag.

"My father used to take me to all the racetracks. He liked to bet on the horses," she said, handing me one of the binoculars. "He even knew some of the jockeys."

"There's nothing to see now. There are no horses," I complained.

"But you can see it, Lucy—the oval track, the green middle against the brown earth, the white railings. Now imagine you see the line of horses. They're jittery at their starting gate. The riders can hardly keep them in. When the gates burst open, their hooves kick up the ground. At the finish line, they stretch themselves long, as if they've sprouted wings, their eyes, blind to the crowds, the noise in the stands. Can you see it?"

I didn't get it, wasn't sure what to say to her. There was nothing out there, no one on the track. "O.K." I mumbled.

"You can see it if you close your eyes, and concentrate."

I could see my mother taking it all in, the smell of the horses, their leather saddles and stirrups, the jockeys' racing silks.

"What are we doing here?"

"I used to do some horseback riding when I was your age, nothing professional, just on the trails around Griffith Park. They are beautiful, aren't they, Lucy?"

Suddenly I understood her. She too had a photographer's eye, laying one image on top of the other, freeing it from its conformity. She knew that what was in the mind's eye was just as powerful as the likeness through the lens. I looked up and I could see the horses now, the hoof marks on the track, the jockeys so low, as if they were part of the horses, as though they'd dug their silks into the horses' flesh.

We walked around for a long time. I could tell Mom didn't want to leave. Someone walked by, and Mom recognized him as a trainer her father had known, and he led us through a side door to watch a couple of horses going through their practice runs. Then he showed us around the paddock and the stables.

Mom and the trainer spoke for a few minutes and I stood off to the side watching her talk to him. I could see she liked the stables less, how she winced each time she heard a hoof against the stable door. I saw the way she stood, how she moved her hands when she talked. I could almost see her grip, low in front of a saddle. I could feel the narrow strap of leather in her hands, the cold bit in the horse's mouth, light and steady.

It was as if she were taking the reins once again.

๛

When we returned that night, she came into my room to check if I was asleep. She first sat on the edge of my bed, careful not to take up too much space; then, she seemed to recall the day, and she made herself wider, crawled under the blanket with me.

"Go to sleep, Lucy."

I didn't want to sleep yet. I also wanted to remember everything I'd seen, the train and the ocean, the horses, their dark nostrils flaring, their flanks, and the oval track. I wanted to recall the towers, first at the train station, then at the track, but the smell of her made me drowsy.

"Why do you have to 'fall' asleep?" I whispered to her. "Why does it have to be a fall?"

It was a question I should have posed to Dad. He would have known the science of falling asleep, or sleeping, not sleeping, the simple biology and mechanics of it. He would have explained it to me. He was the expert, but it seemed right now that I should ask her and not him.

"I don't know," she said sleepily and I thought she wasn't going to give me an answer, but she continued. "Falling is something you do when you let go, a kind of surrender, making peace with yourself. You can't sleep unless you give in to it, let it take you over."

Then I knew she was an expert too, but unlike Dad, not in sleep, but in surrender. She'd spent her entire marriage stitching her own kind of white flag. And it was surrender that had taught her sleep.

Her sleepiness had a smell to it, a wonderful odor. I tried to fight off her fragrance, but I couldn't help myself. It was her mother's potion. I heard her breathing in and out, in and out, and I fell with her into sleep.

Mai

I don't know how long we stayed in the refugee camp. It couldn't have been more than a few weeks, but it dragged on like months to me. People came and went in the barracks, faces changing every few days. We should have left by now, but we couldn't because there was something wrong with our papers, Thanh said, and every morning she stormed off to the camp office and yelled at the administrators about where we would be sent, shaking the stained papers she'd brought from Vietnam. I was sure it was my papers that were the problem. There were only two slashes in the place where "father's name" should have been on my torn birth certificate.

I was the problem, always the problem.

Thanh made me go to the school for the camp children, and I went, but I'd come and go as I pleased. After all, I knew everything I needed to know. Linh had taught me English and she'd taught me well. I knew more than the scrawny teacher. She, too, was a refugee and she had no heart left to teach fifty children who came and went in the small schoolroom they gave her. I was good at numbers too. Thanh had taught me arithmetic. Every day, she'd give me columns of numbers to add because she recognized I had her shopkeeper's head.

Linh seemed better for a while, as if some weight had been lifted from her, and then suddenly one morning she woke up and said it. "Cal-i-for-ni-a."

The word stretched long on her lips.

And it was as though she'd awoken from a coma. She began to read the newspapers, and remembered details, names and addresses. She made notes, and took an interest in the people in our barracks. She even accompanied Thanh to the camp office and helped fill out paperwork.

"Only California," she insisted. "He's there," and she showed me the state on a map she'd found. It had the shape of a crooked arm, bent to hold back the great Pacific. She pointed to the length of green, the Sacramento and San Joaquin Valleys cradled in the heart of the state, surrounded by mountains.

"From the California coast you can look out in the direction from where you came, Mai," she said. "There, you'll always be reminded of your home."

For weeks, Thanh pretended to go along with Linh, humoring her, letting her go off to the camp office to see if we were on one of the U.S. lists, but I knew Thanh secretly ignored Linh's new clarity, as if it was only a storm, a sudden typhoon that would pass through quickly. Thanh had other plans. We'd had French papers once and Thanh was plotting to move us to Paris instead.

I couldn't understand why. Thanh had always railed against Paris. She'd had a list of complaints against the city, so much so as if it were a person and not a place. Mostly, she detested the French capital because it was where the American had taken Linh, but it was more than that—it was where the Paris Agreements had been signed, the pact that had brought about the U.S. pullout, the abandonment of Vietnam. Still, Thanh insisted we should go there, to our relatives there, she explained, but I suspected something else.

Paris was a place of surrender, both Vietnam's and Linh's, and that was exactly why Thanh wanted to go there. She was determined to to put her head back in the lion's mouth, proving that she'd survived defeat.

It was all the same to me—France or America.

The French had built their plantations, their pretty colonnades and balustrades, and then left them to rot. The Americans had done the same—they'd raised their military bases and concrete bunkers, only to desert them. The French and the Americans had both come and gone and had left their scars on the land. Worse, they'd each left other imprints.

Wanting to be like them, not wanting to emulate them, wishing for their love was the worst of the marks they'd left behind.

❧

One afternoon, the barracks were mostly empty, and I walked in on Thanh, her face swelled with anger. She was yelling at Linh.

"Now that you're not confused, your old stubbornness has returned," Thanh accused Linh.

"I don't know what you mean," I heard Linh answer slowly, precisely.

"We're not going to California. You have no right to demand it."

"I will decide for my daughter," Linh persisted.

"And what kind of daughter were you? It was you. You killed your father. You took him away from us. It's your fault he's not here to protect us. You and your craziness," Thanh screamed out at Linh.

"No, it's not true." Linh turned to confront her and I could see she was clear-eyed, like a bird. There was no madness in her.

"You did it," Thanh ranted again.

"No," Linh repeated.

"*Assassin,*" Thanh hissed.

"*Hashshashin,*" Linh said calmly. But then a cloud came over her face.

"What are you saying?" For a moment, it was Thanh who was confused.

"It's not French…the word…it's Arabic…from those who used hashish," Linh said, collapsing onto the floor of the barracks.

I saw the desert drained of color. I imagined dunes in a sandstorm and flapping tents.

Thanh continued to yell.

Stop.

I don't know whether I screamed the word out loud, or if it never left my throat, but I had to stop Thanh. I had to end this new killing.

I walked up to my grandmother and slapped her hard across the face. She looked at me, but didn't seem surprised, and she only put her hand up to her cheek, to where I'd left an ugly welt. She rubbed the redness several times, but it wouldn't go away.

"Don't ever say that again," I threatened, standing over Thanh. "If Linh is a murderer, I can be a murderer too."

Then I went to Linh and helped her to the cot.

Linh never mentioned California again. She went back to confusion, to sleep. I sat with her and tried to make her remember. She was my ward now, mine alone, and like a nursemaid, I fed Linh her own dreams, each memory like spoonfuls of soup to an invalid.

※

He is a student of all the pagodas of the city, the Giac Lam, the Giac Vien with its slated roof. But of all the pagodas in the city, the American loves the Jade Emperor's pagoda the best. He brings his books to the paved courtyard with the turtle pond, to sit under the banyan tree, smell the frangipanis. Four guardians of the Great Diamonds watch over Ngoc Hoang, the Jade Emperor, in the front, while the eighteen-armed Linh of the Five Buddhas guards at the back of the complex.

Linh watches him from the entrance. She loves him there, inside his books, closed away. He doesn't wear the saffron robes of the priests, but he is his own monk in that place, barefoot, incense washed.

In the pagoda, he is one with the temple's gardens and pillars, its tombs and ancestral tablets, carved dragonheads. The American too becomes a pagoda, its eaves twisting and turning heavenward. He is the temple's gilded statues, apart, its joss sticks, burning away into the air in zigzag.

She knows he looks for all his answers in his books and she wishes she too could be a book, that he fall forever under her spell of words and paragraphs, pages and chapters. Mostly his books are about Vietnam. He immerses himself in all the annals of the old kingdoms, the ancient dynas-

ties, the Champas, who built brick towers and filled them with statues. He knows by heart the histories of the Portuguese Catholic missionaries, the vise of French Indochine, the surrender of the French at Dien Bien Phu. He reads about the American-backed Prime Minister Diem and his sister-in-law, the strange Madame Nhu. He speaks Vietnamese, and loves her country more than his own, more than her, as if he is an old soul lost and reincarnated from Vietnam's past, lost, searching for his home among the avenues of tamarind, the terraced rice paddies.

She comes and sits beside him. He retells her the stories of the heroines. He relives the rebellion of the Trung sisters, who, pregnant, rose up against the Chinese rulers in gold-plated armor. Trung Trac and Trung Nhi, along with twelve women generals, captured the citadels in the Red River Delta. He recites the story of Trieu Au, the young woman who took over her dead brother's uprising. Sitting in a glittery palanquin, she led her people into battle even though defeat was imminent. He is excited with his finds, but Linh grows sad, weary with his stories of heroines. For he is blind to her own daring.

Linh remembers the legend of Ling Lac Long Quan, who married the immortal Au Co. She bore him a hundred children and fifty who followed their mother to her mountain domain, while the others joined their father in the Num Hai Soa, and Linh wonders why there is always separation, why there is always a parting of ways.

Today, he is elephant-eyed, graying, his shoulders stooped from some great weight. Suddenly she sees it. Tucked in between the pages of his books are the letters his California wife writes to him. Like bookmarks, they remind him of the pages he wants to reread, revisit.

Linh doesn't like his books anymore. They are only hiding places for his wife's letters, safe havens, harbors for Evelyn's words.

A letter falls to the ground and she catches a glimpse of the uncertain postmark, his wife's neat, upright handwriting, the way it strains across the page as if each line is a journey unto itself. There is betrayal in his wife's words. It is not his betrayal, or hers, but the treason of the words themselves. She uses words to cajole him, to wrap herself around him, find his softest spot. Evelyn too uses language to cast her net, remind him of who awaits him on his homecoming.

He doesn't notice when one letter drops. Linh puts her foot over *it, and picks it up, stuffs it away in the pocket of her dress. The letter is hers now, part of her spoils of war.*

Later, she takes it out, studies the return address, and memorizes it. It might be useful some day, important to know where she is, the woman who is his wife.

Lucy

I t was the end of October, and the dry Santa Anas gusted from
the eastern deserts. It was still fire season and the winds breathed in
fire from the deserts, gathering like hallucinations at the mouths of
the canyons, painting the sky ashen-pink. Strange though, the winds
cleared the valley basin of the summer haze, and the Santa Susanna
Mountains reappeared in the north like a gift...

"When's Dad coming home?" I asked my mother.

"He's delayed. He's stopping for a few days in Paris."

She didn't seem to mind much. All this time he'd been away,
she'd take long showers, and sleep sidewise across their king-size
bed. She didn't seem to be in a hurry anymore and she let me do my
homework on the floor of her bedroom. She'd even stopped cooking
and every night we went out to dinner or ordered pizza delivered to
the house. Then we'd stay up late together and watch Carson.

Heeere's Johnny.

The rainbow curtains flapped open and Doc Severinsen smiled
out beneath a shoe polish mustache.

The night before Halloween, I went to bed and for the first time
I could remember, it happened—I slept the entire night. That night,

I seemed to sleep for days, each hour of the night was like a month of nights. I could feel sleep taking over, carrying me away.

I could have slept through the whole morning.

There were so many dreams.

I dreamed I was going up in an elevator full of people. I was in a tall building, and the elevator rose straight up, from story to story, but each time the doors were released, they opened mid-floor and no one exited.

Hold on. Don't let go.

When the elevator reached the top, the people disappeared and I was alone. Suddenly, the walls of the elevator melted, and only its skeleton remained. It looked like the black grill of a birdcage, a wind gusting through girders, a city of lights below.

Mom touched my face.

"Wake up, Lucy. We're going for a ride," she said.

Half asleep, I looked at her and then at the alarm clock on my nightstand. I thought it would be another one of her new outings, but this seemed different. She was wearing a soft, white blouse, gathered low on the neck and a wide, beaded skirt.

"Where are we going?" I asked.

"I'll tell you in the car," she said. "Why don't you take your camera this time?"

When we got to the freeway, I asked her again, but she didn't answer, and only her lips moved, as though she was debating with herself. Then she smoothed down her skirt, rubbed the tiny, embroidered beads with the palm of her hand, and reached over to touch me.

"I hope it rains," she said, looking out the windshield.

"Why?"

"It's the drought. We need the rain, but…it's going to be O.K."

"What is?" I asked as I looked out the window. It looked like we were heading in the direction of the airport. Maybe Dad had called and was coming home on an earlier flight. I turned to Mom. "Are we going to pick up Dad?"

"No. I lost something," she said, as she was driving. Then she picked up an airline ticket from the car floor and flapped it over the top of the steering wheel.

"What did you lose?"

"It's really kind of stupid, you know, just a pair of gloves. I know they wouldn't have them…it's been so long, but I just have to check in the lost-and-found. I didn't do it then, and I should have. I should have done everything I could, but I didn't understand that it was important. Here. You hold on to it," she said as she handed me the ticket. She then pulled down the visor and looked at herself in the little mirror.

I glanced at the ticket. It was old, smudged. Round trip, Los Angeles to New York, New York to Paris and back.

"I don't understand. It's old, from the Sixties."

"I know. It was when we went on our honeymoon…to Paris."

"Paris?"

I'd heard all the stories about their two-week honeymoon… Mom had kept all the dinner menus and museum ticket stubs. I'd seen the slides of the trip, projected dozens of times in our living room. I remembered the sound of the carousel clicking, and how the tiny slide would expand to fill up the entire wall—my parents at the Arch of Triumph, the Louvre and a café on the Champs-Élysée. I'd go up to the image and stand to the side, tracing the outlines of the monuments with my finger, their images fleeting.

"I think I lost them on the airplane coming back…from Paris," she said. "They were very soft, you know, kidskin. When I'd put them on, I could hardly feel them on my hands. They had little pearl buttons. You don't mind, Lucy, do you?"

"Well…O.K." I said, still unsure.

"Don't worry, it's not just some wild goose chase," she said, but she wasn't trying to be convincing. "You'll understand when we get there."

We arrived at the airport and Mom parked the car near the control tower. Above us, I imagined the air traffic control room, where radars blipped green across dozens of screens, where planes were tracked and signaled home, and the spot seemed to give my mother courage. Nearby was the spider-legged Theme building, looking like a saucer suspended in the sky. We got out of the car and walked toward it. Two parabolic arches intersected above the central pillar rising from its midsection. I stood beneath one of the four legs of the building and took photos from below.

"Those are going to be good," Mom remarked.

"You think so?"

"Yes, because you're taking the photos from the building's foothold, where it begins and ends, the place where the circle is closed," she said.

"You're right," I answered, looking again through the view-finder.

How did you know that, Mom?

"Come, let's go on," she said.

Along the way, she stopped a few people, asking for directions and we found the claims area on the first floor of the TWA terminal. Mom rushed ahead of me in her big, round skirt, past the grinding baggage carousels and the stacks of abandoned luggage, to the small office at the back.

My mother stopped at the counter and caught her breath, plunked down her yellowed tickets.

"I've lost my gloves," she said to a woman in a blue uniform. Behind the counter were three wall clocks displaying the times in Los Angeles, New York, and Paris. The woman looked up and squinted at Mom. Then she took out a clipboard, and handed it to my mother.

"This is a listing of all the items we found in the last two weeks," she chirped. "It's by date and item."

"You don't understand," Mom said, almost beaming as she leaned over the counter. "It was a while ago."

"How long ago, ma'am?"

Mom didn't respond and I looked at my mother closely. She was as beautiful as ever, but more than that, fascinating, gypsy-like. She seemed to have taken on some new wizardry, like a lens blown open to full aperture.

"It was fifteen years ago," I piped in.

"Fifteen years?" the woman said, incredulous. "We wouldn't keep anything for that long."

"Are you sure?" Mom insisted.

I came up to my mother and gave her a hug around the waist. She wasn't crazy. She'd known she wouldn't find her gloves. It wasn't the gloves she was after.

It was something else.

She was finishing something that had been unfinished—Paris and Dad. Something had unraveled then, after their honeymoon, and now she needed to retrace her steps, figure out how to splice it back together, see its evolution, like time-lapse photography.

I looked outside and it had begun to drizzle.

The woman quickly jotted down a telephone number on a piece of paper and gave it to my mother. She could call the central office in New York for more information about the gloves, the lady said, quickly handing her the paper, but Mom didn't take it from her.

"That's all right," Mom said. "I don't need them anymore," she said. "But you know," she continued. "Your clock—it's wrong."

"Clock?" the lady answered, looking behind her.

"Yes. That one." She pointed to one of the clocks on the wall. "The one that shows Paris time. It's wrong. You should fix it," she almost commanded, turning around to leave.

And her big skirt floated up in the air of the automatic door, danced around her, the hundreds of beads flickering like motes in the light of a projector, like veils of forgotten secrets.

Mai

It was raining hard, thundering when we landed at Orly in Paris. Thanh's cousin, Hong, and her husband, Do, picked us up at the airport. Hong was even tinier than Thanh, her blue eye shadow smeared in a thick, uneven layer across her lids. Hong hugged Thanh, and it was the first time I saw my grandmother cry.

Do was a cab driver and we got into the back of his black taxi. Everyone kept looking at me, waiting for my reaction, but I didn't say a word as we drove on the *peripherique*, the highway that circled Paris. I was still quiet when we reached the city limits.

"Well, what do you say about Paris, Mai?" Hong asked me. She expected my eyes to grow wide with the boulevards. She was hinting for me to thank her for sponsoring us.

"I've seen it," I answered, and Hong eyed Thanh, caught Thanh's look of disapproval.

I wasn't ungrateful. It was just that they didn't understand. Paris was nothing new to me, its quays and churches, the river that cut it in half. I'd been to Paris a hundred times with Linh. I'd seen the orange-roofed Place des Vosges, its fountains and the precision of its windows. I'd already marveled at the obelisk of the Concorde, and read its hieroglyphics, felt their etchings into the stone.

The city was nothing I hadn't seen in Linh's dreams.

Linh suddenly gasped next to me. For a moment, I was hopeful. I thought she'd recognized something that would wake her once more out of her sadness, like the time she'd said "California" in the barracks, but it was the news on the radio she'd heard, a bulletin that an American had been electrocuted in a puddle of water during the electrical storm in the Tuileries Gardens. She looked out the window for a moment.

"*Il pleut,*" Linh said, sitting back and closing her eyes.

It's raining.

"*Pleut, Pleurer,*" she said.

And those were the last two words I heard Linh utter.

We reached Hong's apartment and Do carried our three small bags up the narrow stairs. I looked around the apartment trying to find something that reminded me of my homeland, but there was nothing. Hong and Do had left Vietnam soon after the French had been defeated. They'd lived in Paris for twenty years and there was nothing of open windows and breezes, dark woods and rattan. There was no smell of spice. It was all closed, spindly, gilded furniture, wide-striped divans and heavy curtains, the windows shut tightly.

They were French by now, their lips parting fast, cold.

There was nothing of slowness here.

Even the water in the kitchen poured out too fast, noisy.

"Come, I'll show you to your rooms," Hong motioned for us to follow her. "You each have a room…of your own," she continued, and she seemed pleased to be the mistress of our new bounty.

After a few weeks, Thanh got a job as a bookkeeper for a French bakery in the fourteenth *arrondissement*. Every night, she'd bring long, green ledger books back home with her from work. I'd never seen her happier, sitting beneath the chandelier of Hong's dining room, writing and erasing, blowing her erasures off the thin columns. She whistled like a child.

She had her numbers back now.

To help with expenses, Linh cleaned apartments in Hong's building. I hated seeing Linh on her knees, scrubbing French people's bidets and toilets, but Linh didn't seem to mind. She'd stopped talking by then, and used only sign language. I don't know where she learned to sign in French, but it was her hands that danced her words for her now. Her hands were in constant motion, sometimes furious, at other times slow. All the words that had gradually abandoned her over the years, had now come back to her in her hands. She was as voiceless as the silent letters, the strange anomalies of English and French, which appeared in a word, bearing no sound.

I watched her, studied her hands closely and I became the only one who could understand what she was saying.

I was indifferent to Paris. It was cold, rainy, but it didn't take me long to get used to the city, the maze of streets and cars. I bought a *carte d'orange* pass for the Metro and felt at home in the fluorescent light of the stations, and the steaming underground tunnels snaking under the city. I'd wait for the train on the track, hear its distant rumble as the beast rushed nearer to me, the train doors then sliding open, sucking me inside. I liked the lights in the train, the way they robbed everything of color, the way they made everyone indistinct.

I memorized the Metro map. Soon I knew every stop on all the routes. Every line had a beginning and an end, and that was good. There was no opportunity for the train to stray somewhere unexpected, somewhere it shouldn't. I liked the curve of the tiled ceilings, the steps that led me deeper into the labyrinth of tunnels, and the press of the wooden turnstiles on my hips.

No one bothered me down there, or asked me questions. It was different in the subway. It all seemed recognizable to me—the comings and goings, passing through, and not staying put.

I watched the pickpockets, learned their techniques. I'd stolen before, cigarettes and oranges, but it wasn't the same gliding my hand into someone's coat, so close to their skin. I had to do it, to see how it felt, how Linh had felt when she stole Evelyn's letter from her American's book.

Each station, every stop had its own personality. The central

Concorde station burst with merging platforms. The Porte de Saint Cloud, the last station in the southwest was quiet, lonely at the tunnel's end.

The best was watching the trains disgorging their passengers—waves of people filling up the station and then none, like the tide on a beach.

At night, I'd come back and tell Linh about my journeys and she listened to my stories.

"I brought you something," I told her, one night.

I collected for her lost things, items that had fallen out of people's pockets and bags, things that had found their way to the floor. I retrieved ticket stubs and combs, glasses and gloves, as though souvenirs from a happy excursion. I took them each night out of my school bag and brought them to her, because I knew it was only broken things, the shreds, left over, that could make her whole again.

⚘

The American finds Linh asleep on his hotel floor. He believes her when she tells him she's fallen off the bed in her sleep and picks her up in his arms, brings her back to the bed. She doesn't tell him she hasn't fallen, that she sometimes makes her way down to the floor on purpose.

She finds herself among the cracks, the crevices of the floor. She presses her body, compresses it down, each bone, bone to tile, to make peace with gravity, with all things fallen.

"Come to bed, Linh."

The American should have left her, he should have left her then, the night he found her on the floor, the night her mind left, journeyed without her.

Leave me.

She doesn't want his pity, his doctoring. She doesn't want him to see her like that. But he doesn't leave her this night.

"Sleep, Linh."

"No. Let me tell you about the Perfume Pagoda. That will make me well."

Upstream on the Swallow River is the temple, the Perfume Pagoda. It is built into the limestone cliffs of the Mountain of Fragrant Traces.

It is a cluster of caverns under the mossy cliffs, the blue-mist mountains of the North.

Take me there.

Linh wants to reach up to catch the drops of water from the stalactites, mother's milk to heal all sorrows, sickness. She wants to make an offering to the spirits, in the grottoes that are red, angry with fires.

"I'll take you. I promise."

It was where male is transformed into female, and the Goddess of Compassion is born.

It is where fallen things find their home, things dropped and forgotten and promises not kept.

Mai

Once, Linh followed me to the Metro and from that moment on, it was all she wanted—to ride the subway with me for hours. Every Sunday, it was the same—we'd begin at the *Concorde* at the center of the city, and ride out to the edges of Paris, then back to the center again to find another rail line.

Back and forth, Linh couldn't get enough of the Metro, the oil on its rails, its fume was her new oxygen.

At the outset, she wouldn't exit the station at the last stop. She'd run back through the turnstile, and we'd return. But soon, she agreed to stop at every station, leaving the car for only for a moment, then back on the same train. After a while, I persuaded her to stay and linger on the platform. She paced to and fro, touching the benches, looking up at the giant concave posters on the walls. Like a woman choosing fruit in a market, she studied the Metro map, its web of stops, as if she were looking for something, some perfect place. She traced the stations with her finger, tapping on those named for great battles—Austerlitz, Stalingrad, Bir Hakeim, as though they were her battles, her victories and defeats. She pored over the map, like a soldier charting troop movements and land mines.

I played along with her. It didn't matter to me whether we were at the Mairie d'Ivry or the Pont de Sevres, the Madeleine or the Palais Royal, but it mattered now to Linh, as though the choice of a station was an argument, a point to be defended on her unfinished thesis.

I could see her mouthing the names of the stops, separating them into syllables—Lu-xem-bourg, Plai-ssance, Cle-men-ceau.

No, she shook her head, then took out a pen and wrote me a note on a pad she kept in her pocket.

It's not the right one.

She especially liked the stations that connected with the trains, the *gares* where long, passenger trains departed for the south of France or Belgium in the north. She'd go up to peek into the first-class compartments, the dining cars, but she wouldn't board any train that ran above ground. She'd wander off sometimes, but I watched her carefully, and made sure I didn't lose her.

It was the tunnels that made Linh soft again, melting, like candy.

Sometimes, late at night, she'd take my hand and we'd run together down the corridors.

Come.

She was looking for something.

Each time a train rumbled down the track, the platform vibrating beneath her feet was a heartbeat and her mouth moved like honey. Two trains crossed each other's path, then separated in opposite directions, and I saw the pulse throb in her temple.

She was best here, at home, fluid, and at each station she left her own marker, a tiny "L" she scratched out with a coin at the very edge of the platform, the final centimeter before the landing fell into nothingness.

In the end, I convinced her to walk up the stairs to the streets at the end of each of the rail lines. We'd walk around the working-class neighborhoods, the streets where few tourists ventured. We found Vaugirard, where first floor windows looked onto gritty streets, but fluttered with freshly pressed curtains.

At the Abbesses, we sat and watched the commuters come out of the station onto a circular place of trees and benches. She liked to stand beneath the curve of ironwork that spelled out "Metropolitan." We'd walk over to the funicular, its rails a mirror of the steps that led up to the blinding white of the Sacré Coeur.

Once, I took her to a little restaurant near Pigalle, where the Tunisians lived, and we both ate lemon-colored couscous. She looked beautiful that day, sylphlike, her hair swept up in a hat, her dress crisply ironed.

"You can take off your hat," I said to her, as we sat down at the table.

She shook her head no, and then wrote me a note:

It holds my thoughts.

We sat for a while and watched the people coming home from work with their fishnet bags of groceries. She took a paper napkin from the table and wrote furiously. I asked to look at it and I saw she'd filled it to its edges with symbols of pronunciation, marks and special signs, abbreviations. She took another and the second napkin soon became full with question marks and ellipses, hyphens and dashes.

There are no more questions now, she had written down.

A waiter came by. She ordered sweet Orangina and I ordered the same. I thought maybe there was finally the color of sunset between us, a truce of orange.

But Linh proved me wrong.

A few days later, I offered to take her to the Metro, but she refused me. I asked her again, remembering our times there, but she only shook her head and smiled.

Had she found what she was looking for?

⌘

It is the week of Tet and Cay-Neu offerings are planted. The bamboo sticks are decorated with pineapple leaves and cocks' feathers, red paper, special candles, and lanterns to chase away the evil spirits. Grandfather's house is full of fresh flowers and Grandfather buys the best French brandy and champagne, and Russian caviar, to celebrate the New Year.

All through the house, there is the aroma of banana leaves and sweet rice cakes, Banh Chung. The seeds of the lotus flower are boiled into sweet bean soup and the cook makes crème caramel. Thanh makes a trip to the cemetery to invite the spirits of dead relatives and Linh dresses in her best tunic. Linh takes the American to the Cho Lon district in the west of the city where vendors sell caged birds and banners, and wrought-iron balconies extend from second-story windows. They pass the closed sandal shops and watch the dragon dances, the fire-eaters in the street. Incense and smoke fill the air, and fireworks explode, lighting up the night sky.

They go back to his room at the hotel, Tet's fragrant incense still in their hair. He wakes up in the middle of the night and tells her his dreams.

The American is best in the night.

His voice is different, his breath in her ear. He is silk, softened and loosened, then spun; he is lacquer and mother of pearl inlay, dense and smooth; he is the glaze of cobalt blue, a woodcut. He dreams of mystical beasts and winged horses, wrinkled elephants with missing tusks, crying great tears. They wear their sadness in their yellowing, ivory tusks. Sharp-toothed, the animals take him on journeys to the ancient temples overrun, suffocated by the gangrene of the jungle, where bells, clogged by vines, no longer ring. She rides with him on a flying horse, floats with him in a sampan down muddy rivers, hears the boatman's rowing song.

That night, his hands are different, smaller. They don't listen to the mandates of the operating room. They forget all surgical procedures and techniques. They are imprecise, imperfect at night. They only listen to her. She wishes his hands would always be that way. Linh wants his hands all to herself. Linh says a silent prayer asking the princess of the Perfume Pagoda for guidance. The princess knows about love, about hands. Against her father's will, the princess chose to retreat to a cave. But when her father's hands became diseased with leprosy, the princess of the Perfume Pagoda sacrificed her own hands to heal her father's.

When she finishes her prayer, Linh is afraid. She's done something bad. It is wrong to wish that he never hold a scalpel again.

She listens again, lets him tell her his dreams, but she knows them all. She knows them because she's been the one weaving them all along, her midnight gifts like the silkworm's cocoons, for him to unravel.

Lucy

ॐ

The moment I woke up, I knew I would go there.

Come to the river.

The thought stayed with me, a part of a dream that wouldn't let go, and it crossed over from night into the porous morning.

It was less than a mile from our house, only steps from my school, Grant High, but I'd never been down there before. I'd thought it was just a concrete ditch until Dad told me it was part of the Los Angeles River. In the mid-thirties, the Army Corps of Engineers began pouring concrete into the river's bed, he'd said, to tame the surge of water that would sweep over its banks once in a decade, and over the course of twenty years, what began as a renegade river, became a phantom watercourse.

Everyone in the valley called it "the wash," and I'd seen glimpses of it when I was in the car. Suddenly I'd see it—a long, open tunnel, almost a canyon beneath the street—an emptiness below. The water appeared and disappeared, but I hadn't thought about it for a long time.

Come now.

"Don't pick me up after school today," I told Mom. "I need to go to the library," I said, making up an excuse.

"I can pick you up later," Mom offered.

"No, it's O.K., I'll get a ride."

After the last class, I put all my books away neatly in my locker and waited for the hallways to empty. I walked outside and it was there, across the street from the track, fenced off with chain link and barbed wire.

No Trespassing.

"It's dangerous. Don't ever go down there," Mom had warned me my first day of high school, but there had been almost a wistfulness in her voice, a craving more than a dreading. I had to see the river. Not from above, but from below, from its inside.

Come, I'm here.

Near the fence, there were crumpled candy bar wrappers, and beyond that, the sound of crickets. On the other side, one man leaned back hard against the fence. On the other side, a woman curled two fingers around a metal link, snapping the fence back to see if it moved, and it did. It rattled in her hands, back and forth, like a giant cage.

I walked for a while, found a small opening, and then slipped through a gap between one of the padlocked gates.

I could see it better now. The riverbed wasn't really flat. There was a smaller alleyway cut into the center of the concrete like a train track. I almost turned back. I didn't know what I was doing here, in this river, this ugly subway of concrete.

Climbing down the embankment, I could hear the cars above, like reeds rushing and sucking out the air. I should have been scared, frightened of the water that was sometimes released from the aqueducts in the north without warning. And when the rains came, every drop of water from the eastern edge of the city to the west, every creek and spring and melting snow-pack barreled into the river.

I was sure someone would have seen me by now, stealing in here like a burglar, but no one came.

I looked around. Somewhere to the north was a maze of channels, unseen reservoirs, dams, catch basins, and pumping stations.

The river.

I stopped. A pair of shoes sat prettily near the edge, the heels wet with a slow trickle of moss-green water. Some woman had left them, twin landmarks in matted suede, like the river's own suicide note.

I was here.

Further down, I reached the bottom and started walking. Away from school, the colored murals depicting L.A.'s history were gone, the wash now backing up into large blocks of apartment complexes. All the windows were small, openings half-closed, squinting to forget the river alongside them. The strips of green that had bordered the river had disappeared into an alternate universe. The mass of gray took out all the hues, rendering it colorless. Like infra-red film, it reversed shadow, turning night into day; the sky darkened, the landscape, luminous and moonlit. As I was walking, I felt a misalignment. I looked down and saw that one of the shoelaces on my sneakers was tightly tied, the other loose and I had a choice—to unloosen the one that was tied, or to refasten the one that was slack.

The sky split, a drop of rain fell on my forehead and I untied the one that had been secure, let it slip to the ground and muddy itself. I remembered last winter, when the rains thundered through the storm channels, churning in a torrent, and suddenly I couldn't catch my breath, but a patch of grass erupted wildly in a defiant green from the cement and I knew nothing would happen to me here, in the bed of this river. The water was only a ghost, a memory.

Close your eyes.

There were branches strewn and debris, wadded-up papers. I lost my bearings. Was I still beneath Burbank Boulevard heading north or had the channel shifted, curved east now?

There was no north, no south here.

The river cut the land, making its own borders.

The trickle of water was bigger now.

Suddenly, I was tired and wanted to lie down, to rest my head on the concrete.

"Lucy."

Her voice was barely audible, as if she were waking me up in the morning. She'd known where to find me and I saw Mom standing

above me, a simple silhouette. It was late now and only the edge of
her sweater glowed with the last bit of light.

"Lucy, please," my mother yelled out now, shaking the fence
like a prisoner.

But it's the river that's in chains.

"I'm coming, Mom."

I searched my jacket pockets. I wanted to leave something
behind before I left, a token, like the woman who'd left her shoes.
There was only a movie stub, torn in half from the day before. The
attendant had somehow ripped them exactly in half, each a reflection of the other, and I had kept them both thinking maybe I'd tape
them back together.

I looked at the stubs, and threw them into the trickle of water.
I left their union to this river.

"My Lucy," Mom cried out again.

I looked up at her. I'd made my pilgrimage and I could leave
now. It was her voice that was water, my mother's voice, and I climbed
up the embankment, to join her.

Mai

I attended the *lycée* near Hong's apartment, but every morning before I left for school I checked on Linh. She was up all night now, falling asleep only when I got up to leave. Tiny in the bed, each morning she faded smaller and smaller. Everything was ebbing from her, shrinking, even her dreams.

School was easy. I didn't have to break my head on conjugations like the others. Linh had taught me that long ago. French was simple, it was a grid of roots and rules. It wasn't like English, with all its exceptions, its beautiful disarray. Mathematics wasn't any harder. I'd come from a place of divided things, a country of additions and subtractions. Intersecting lines and borders moved and removed—they were all familiar to me.

※

I decided I didn't want to come directly home after school and found a job selling drinks to the tourists who got off the buses near the Eiffel Tower. The buses were raucous red, driving round the city from one monument to the other. I carried cold sodas in a cooler slung over my shoulder and sold them for one Franc less than the price at the snack bar near the *pilier sud*. I was good at spotting potential customers as they stepped off the bus, and sold out my cooler quicker than any of the other hawkers.

Besides the Metro, the Eiffel Tower was the only place I could abide. Its black feet took hold of the ground, grabbed onto it, and the tower itself seemed like a mountain of black iron. But it also stood like a lady, delicate and lacy, and I admired its contradictions.

I'd found her, my Black Lady Mountain.

The tourists waited patiently in line for hours to walk up the stairs or take the elevator to look down from its heights, but I liked to stand beneath the tower's belly, and look up, feeling myself rising. I didn't like looking at the tower from any part of the city, making sure I avoided its spire in the distance. I only wanted to see it from below, from its girth and strength, where it gave the impression that it would never fall. Sometimes, I wished they'd drape it over with giant tarps, cover it up and leave me in there, in its heavenly dark.

It was there that I met Nguyen. One afternoon I noticed someone staring at me from one of the benches, open-mouthed as if he'd seen a phantom. I didn't know what he could be looking at. I was only in my school uniform, my white blouse and blue skirt. Thanh had made me cut my hair short and I was no beauty, but I moved and he moved closer. I ran off that first afternoon, but returned the next day. I knew he'd be there, waiting for me. We spoke and he told me he was nineteen, but I knew I was older than him because my wrongdoings had aged me beyond my years.

"I'm named for the great poet Nguyen Trai," he announced. "Tell me your name."

"No," I said.

"Why?"

"A name tells too much."

For weeks, I barely talked to him. Still, he'd meet me there, at the tower, every day after school. He had beautiful eyes, and I wanted to touch his face, even kiss him, but I waited for the right time.

After a few weeks, I let him kiss me against the cold of the tower's metal, his warm hand beneath my white blouse, his mouth perfect on mine.

"Tell me your name now," he asked again.

"I am Linh," I lied to him.

"And where do you come from, where do you live?"

"I can see the river from my window," I lied again, knowing Hong's apartment was on the edge of the city, nowhere near its artery, the Seine.

He smiled. I knew he'd followed me home once, and he knew exactly where I lived, but he seemed to enjoy my fabrications.

"Walk up there with me," he challenged me, and pointed to the top. He thought he could hypnotize me with the tower, that it would give him a way of winning me over.

"No." I didn't want to make the climb, and admit that the tower grew narrower as it rose.

"Are you frightened of heights?"

"It doesn't scare me," I lied once more, but it was a different fear that plagued me. I was afraid of reaching the top, and tossing myself over, like the woman of Black Lady Mountain.

I thought he'd ask me again, but he didn't, and I liked his restraint.

I knew I had to meet the challenge, though—without Nguyen.

That day, after I thought he'd gone home, I bought a ticket and walked up the stairs, grabbing on to the railing. Halfway up the tower, I looked out, and saw the city spread out like a quilt below me. I looked down and saw Nguyen had returned. He was watching me from below.

"My name is Mai," I yelled down, thinking he was too far to hear, but I was mistaken.

"Mai," he called out to me, and I liked the sound of my name, pronounced twice.

Then I took the last elevator to the highest point, where the tower peaked, gathering light and electricity. I saw her power to take in signals and prayers, dreams, like a beacon. It was there I made peace with the Lady.

⁊⥿

Northwest of Saigon and three thousand feet above the rice paddies rises Nui Ba Den, peaking from the empty flatlands.

Linh travels there alone, without him.

The roads are dangerous by then, the bombers have sprayed Agent Orange, poisoned the trails with venom, ripping the green out from the land. There are no travelers on the main roads of jeeps, convoys, and tanks. She pays someone to take her on the back roads.

She reaches the base. Linh is breathless as she walks up, cold, to the mountain shrine. On the way are the cave-temples where pilgrims come to pay homage to the legend of Black Lady Mountain. She brings no food, only candles and joss from the bark of the boi loi tree to mark the journey. It is the last pilgrimage she will make in this land.

Halfway up is the Van Son Pagoda, adorning the mountain like a pearl. Most of the pilgrims walk no further, but Linh keeps walking, pledging to reach the top. She takes her shoes off to walk faster. It is the top that she must reach, to its mercifulness and the candor of its view.

Two hours past the pagoda, and a wind knocks her to the ground.

A hundred memories gather like clouds at sunset, then disappear. She can almost taste them, their faint reflections. She wants to capture them, but they retreat, and flee, slipping away like vapor.

When she awakes, she is at the bottom of Black Lady Mountain, her shoes by her side. Someone has carried her down and placed her gently there.

Mai

A cold, hard light filtered in from the kitchen window as Thanh and Hong sat and peeled hardboiled eggs on the table. They knocked the eggs into the rim of a large, oval plate, then plucked the shells from the hardened, white inside. All around them a heap of cracked shells, delicate shards, covered the table.

They were counting the eggs when I told them about Nguyen.

"He says he loves me," I announced. "And I've invited him here to meet you."

"How can he love you? Anyway, you're just a child," Thanh laughed.

Hong said I shouldn't have anything to do with someone I'd met under the Eiffel Tower, but I knew she'd change her mind.

"It's too late to call him," I devised. "You can tell him yourself when he comes."

The buzzer rang and I saw Thanh's eyes almost light up the dark hallway. He introduced himself, and I could tell Thanh admired his fine, tailored clothes from the Rue de Rivoli, his glove-leather shoes. She was factoring in his silky socks, adding it to her equation.

The two women threw their aprons onto the kitchen table and straightened their skirts. We all sat down in Cousin Hong's salon of stretched silk walls, and she served espresso with lemon peel in her best, gold-rimmed cups.

"I'm studying mythology at the Sorbonne," Nguyen said, taking a sip of the espresso.

"Mmm, mythology," Thanh hummed. "And what does your father do?"

"He's a doctor," Nguyen responded.

"Ah, *un medecin aussi*," Cousin Hong mewed, as though that gave Nguyen and myself something in common.

Hong sent Do to the patisserie across the street. He brought back pastries and sweet cakes and Hong put them out on enamel cake stands. It was raining now, and a lightning storm crackled over the roofs of the city. Linh wandered into the room and she seemed upset, pacing back and forth. She walked to the window while Thanh and Hong continued to question Nguyen.

"Where do you live?" Hong pulled up her chair closer to Nguyen.

"On the Avenue Mozart."

"Ah, Mozart." Hong and Thanh sang in unison.

"More coffee?"

No one noticed when Linh walked over to the window and pulled back the curtains. She looked toward me and caught my eye. Her index finger and thumb formed an "L," then three more letters I couldn't make out.

I smiled at her but then turned away to listen to the others talking. I wanted to see how Nguyen behaved with Thanh and Hong. They would do a good job of testing his mettle, I thought. I didn't notice that when Linh left the room she had shut the apartment door behind her.

Two hours later, Linh hadn't returned.

"She's wandered away before. She'll come back," Hong predicted.

"We should call the police," I said.

"No need to involve them. I'll go out and look for her myself," Thanh said, putting on her coat.

"No, it's different this time," I insisted. I could see now the letters Linh had signed just before she'd left.

She'd spelled out her name, like a signature at the end of a page, a goodbye, and I was sure she wouldn't come back.

"Stay with Mai," Thanh said to Nguyen.

"No, I'm going to look for her," and we all searched the nearby streets, Do and Thanh in his cab, Nguyen and I in Nguyen's green Fiat.

Night fell, and Thanh finally relented. She went to the police station and filed a missing person's report but the tired officer at the police station shook his head at us and said not to expect to find her. It was easy to vanish in a city like Paris, he said.

Thanh and Do returned home, but I refused to stop looking for Linh. I thought about the places she might go.

"Maybe she didn't want to disappear, and she only wants to find a place to sleep," I said to Nguyen in the car. I told him about our rides on the Metro.

"We'll go there," he offered, and he parked his car.

We went from station to station until the last train left, but there was no sign of her. I thought of all the other places that might draw her in. We went to a place near the Luxembourg Gardens, where the birds swept in, where their feathers floated down like snow. There was another spot beneath the Pont Neuf, under the eye of the Saint Chapelle. Maybe she'd found her way to the antique booksellers, closed now on the quay.

They were places Linh would have liked, places I would have gone if I wanted to find a place to fall asleep.

But she wasn't in any of those places either.

Nguyen left me at the steps of the apartment.

"We'll find her," he said, hopefully.

"We won't."

꙰

I went to Linh's room and sat down on her bed. She was gone, but she'd left her imprint on the sheets. I could still smell her, her scent was in the room. I pounded on Linh's bare bed. It was my fault she'd disappeared to reclaim her memories. I'd wrested them away from her and left her with only their husk.

I curled up on Linh's bed and asked her to forgive me. Then I tried to remember, giving her back every memory I'd bootlegged from her. Like a maid laying out her mistress's dresses, one by one, I laid out her favorite dreams on the bedspread for her to see and count. I wanted her to be sure, certain I hadn't cheated her of even one of her dreams.

Please, Linh. Take my offering. Come back to me.

Mai

I t was a month since Linh had disappeared and I couldn't sleep at night anymore, and only in little snatches of sleep during the day. Nguyen was worried about me and came to see me after his classes each evening.

One night, we sat in the salon and Hong turned on the television set to watch the Eurovision song contest. They were about to announce the winners when the telephone rang and Thanh picked up the phone.

I couldn't hear the voice on the other end, but I knew.

It was Linh's American.

Thanh held up the receiver over her head.

It was him.

"You are here...in Paris?" she asked him. "Linh is missing," she told him.

Why had he come now?

Linh had waited so long and it was not right that he would call now that she was gone. I pretended I didn't care, but I listened closely as my grandmother spoke then hung up the telephone and described her conversation.

Linh's American had said he'd been trying to find us for months. He'd just been to Vietnam and had finally tracked us down through the Red Cross.

He wanted to see me.

"He says he wants to take you to Los Angeles," Thanh repeated her exchange. "But I won't let him," she growled, and the sound reminded me of the stray dogs of Saigon, the way they howled in the night. "He ruined Linh, but I'm not going to let him do it to you."

She was mistaken. Only I could ruin myself, and had done so already, but I kept my mouth shut, because I wondered how it would all turn out, as though she was talking about someone else, another girl. That was nothing new to me. I'd always felt that way, as if I was myself, but also someone else as well, never one, but two.

It was no surprise when Cousin Hong immediately disagreed with Thanh. She had made a habit of interfering. It was the price Thanh paid for Hong's extended hospitality. From the moment we'd come to live with her, she thought she had a say in our decisions, our business.

And this was just business to Thanh.

Where I would go and if I would go was a matter of numbers, nothing more, I knew as I saw Thanh and Hong huddled together, figuring, peddling. I was damaged goods, just part of the long tally sheet of what was owed. I was red ink, an entry on one of Thanh's greenish ledger sheets and Thanh wanted to collect.

Hong said I was meant to see him, destined to go to California. She kept repeating the word "California" over and over again and I could see my grandmother's neck tighten into a hundred knots. I knew Thanh would never admit her guilt. California was the last word Linh had spoken that time in the barracks, when she'd been in her right mind. It was the last word she'd uttered before Thanh had stolen Linh's sanity with her accusations.

Do looked at me but didn't say a thing. I appreciated his silence and quiet kindnesses to me. Every morning, he'd slip me five Francs before he dropped me off at the *lycée*. After school, he'd pick me up to drive around the city to look for Linh. Sometimes, we'd drive into the night, the top of his taxi glowing like a firefly.

He'd tell me about being a driver, about the passengers who sometimes talked to themselves, the couples who slammed the door of his cab, arguing; the others who kissed in the back seat as if he weren't there. He was used to the sliding window between him and his customers, used to being invisible and keeping his opinions to himself, and I followed his example, keeping quiet about my reason for going to California. I wasn't going for myself, to reclaim my father, but I would get him back—for Linh's sake.

The argument between Thanh and Hong continued for days, but it was Nguyen who ended it. He'd been coming over and sitting with us every night since Linh's disappearance. Hong had made him part of the family, and even insisted he sit on Do's favorite chair in the salon. But I became wary of Nguyen. He wasn't the same, now that he was conscripted into the family's service, now that they fussed and smiled every time he came to the apartment door.

"She should go to California, and I will go with her," he announced.

"I'm not sure...." Thanh began.

"Maybe seeing her father will help her sleep," Nguyen interrupted her. "She must go."

"If she goes, she will never come back to us," Thanh continued.

"I have an uncle in Orange County and we can stay with him," Nguyen persisted. "She doesn't have to stay with her father."

"Then, I will let her go," Thanh said, suddenly capitulating, but I wasn't sure why.

Was it me or Linh she was releasing?

※

A few days later, we went to meet Linh's American in the back room of a small restaurant on the Left Bank. Thanh and Hong dressed up, as if to mark a special occasion. Nguyen, too, wore his best, a black suit and tie. Only I argued with Thanh about wearing a dress, but I was happy we were meeting at a Vietnamese restaurant. Linh's American would be forced to take in the smells of lotus flower and squid, the fishy *nuoc mam*, to inhale them. He'd have to recall the sounds of reeds and bamboo, rice and water. He'd be forced to remember.

143

Remember what you lost there.

We arrived before him, and sat down and waited. When he came into the room, he walked over to hug me, but I didn't stand up, and he gathered the empty space above me as if he was embracing a spirit.

"Mm…Mai," he stammered on my name, and I relished his frailty.

He was only a faint memory to me, but I recognized his voice, his words, the way he moved his hands. Even though I'd forgotten much of Linh's dreams, her stories, there were still some things I remembered, little shards pricking me. But the longer she was gone, the less I remembered.

Maybe Linh loved you. But I hate you.

He sat down at the table with us. The American's long legs stretched under the small table and bumped up from underneath. He spoke to Thanh and Nguyen, and then turned to the side to steal a look at me, but I expected that. I expected him to look at me, make calculations in his head as to what part of me belonged to Linh and what belonged to him. I could see him doing that. After all, he was a doctor with a head for anatomy, for parts.

He talked about Los Angeles and his house in the valley. He told us about Lucy and said she was not much older than I.

Lucy. He said her name and it lit up a flame inside me.

I didn't know your name. I never knew it was Lucy.

It's you I want to see.

Even Thanh bit her lip, and spoke politely with the American, but I noticed he sat on his hands, and hid them from my prying eyes.

"I'm not a surgeon anymore," he said, and he described how he helped people sleep. Nguyen sat up and looked as though the goddesses he loved so much had risen from their ancient sleep, as though the Fates had shot their bittersweet arrow into the restaurant.

I didn't speak up and tell Nguyen he was wrong, that Linh's American would never be the one to return my sleep to me. It didn't matter that he was a doctor, or even a specialist in sleep medicine. He wouldn't be the one. I hadn't met a man yet who put a woman at ease. It was a woman's job, and I knew now exactly who she would be.

Lucy.

"This is for you." He brought me a gift wrapped in a long, velvet box. Thanh watched me closely as I opened it. I knew she thought it was my duty to show him I didn't want anything from him.

It was a watch and Thanh's satisfaction climbed like a gecko up her face when I snapped the lid shut, pushed it aside on the table. Then I reached out and took it back.

"*Merci*," I said, first to punish Thanh. "Thank you," I said again, this time to let him know.

Linh loved you.

I don't hate you.

I tried to sleep that night, but just like the other nights since Linh ran off, I couldn't. It was Linh's retribution for the dreams I'd stolen from her; now she was paying me back in full by retaking them for herself.

She was the robber now.

I knew what she was doing, her clever plan. I couldn't sleep now, with Linh gone, wandering the streets. There would be no more dreams of her American, of her. And if I couldn't sleep, I couldn't dream.

I wanted to see her sleep again, see her body move like a river and her eyelids soften. If only I could breathe in her hair, like dark honey on her pillow. I longed to see the pretty sight of her, like paper fluttering in the wind.

I needed her voice, to hear her tell me about the words, their context. I wanted to hear her say again how every situation called for its own language and how it adapted to the occasion for which it was used. I wished she'd cast her spell to let me know what form of language, what shape, what measure I could invoke that would bring her back to me.

Like a holy man summoning ancestors, I called out to her dreams to lead me to her, but I'd forgotten them all. Her sleep, her dreams, all sleep ran from me.

Lucy

Mom and I drove to the airport to pick up Dad, but his Air France flight was late. At the gate, Mom drank two cups of coffee from a large Styrofoam cup, each time leaving nervous teeth marks and lipstick on the rim. I sat down near the wide plate windows until his plane taxied to the gate. Then I saw the accordion-like ramp come around and reach out to join the door of the plane. He was last to exit, but I didn't recognize him right away, and he seemed to bring in the fog that always hovered above the airport. Somehow, he didn't look as tall as I remembered.

"It's good to be back," were his first words.

He kissed Mom and then me, and I noticed he smelled faintly of ginger. The rest of the passengers hurried out of the gate area toward the baggage claim, and in a few minutes it was emptied of people. Dad had only a carry-on suitcase and he kneeled down on the carpeted floor, opening it.

"I have presents for both of you," Dad said, handing one package to me, another to Mom.

"What, now?" My mother was puzzled. "It can wait."

"No, now," Dad insisted, like an anxious suitor. "I want you to see what I bought for you."

My mother and I sat down and unwrapped the gifts. He'd brought me a ten-inch replica of the Eiffel Tower; for Mom he'd bought a large bottle of Chanel.

The package slipped out of Mom's hands.

I could see he hadn't meant it.

"The duty free shop must have made a mistake," he stammered.

Mom doesn't wear Chanel—she only wears White Shoulders.

"I'm sorry," he apologized, but too late. Mom ran ahead to the car.

When we reached the parking lot, Mom wanted to drive, but Dad insisted and she gave in, letting him slide into the driver's seat. I watched them from the back. He turned when he spoke to her, but she stared straight ahead and they talked in half sentences, a secret code between them. Dad turned on the radio and I stopped trying to listen, looking only out the window. Far out in the Pacific a distant storm was heading toward Los Angeles, the weather report said, and the air seemed compressed.

Why did you come back?

"I'm going to wash the car," Dad announced when he pulled into our driveway. He immediately dropped his bag in the hallway and took out a bucket from underneath the kitchen sink, filling it with soapy water.

"Dad, aren't you tired?"

"No, I'm fine," he answered, taking the bucket out to the car.

"It's going to rain tonight," Mom remarked, but we both knew it didn't matter to Dad. Washing the car was what he'd always done first thing, every time he'd come home on leave from Vietnam. He'd scrub it down, as if in ablution, washing himself down, removing all trace of where he'd been, what he'd seen.

"I'm not tired at all. This is good," he said as he sprayed the car with the garden hose. Then he spent the entire afternoon soaping it with a sponge, drying it carefully with a yellow chamois, waxing, then shining up the tires with Armor All.

148

By the time I woke up the next day, he was already up, out in the garage at the back of the house, going through old medical journals. I watched him from the open window in the kitchen and saw him leafing through the index of each journal.

I could see he didn't notice Mom's stack of magazines, the back issues of *Life* she'd saved during the war. I'd come across them a week ago.

A U.S. Family Faces Vietnam.

Up Hill 881 with the Marines.

That's where I'd read about Charlie Company, and learned a new vocabulary; words like platoon and bunker, bivouac. But there was something else—I found myself poring over the pages of photographs. They were different from mine—untouched, undoctored. Raw, they were photographs that documented, photo-essays. They were images of encounter, glimpses of the mundane, collaborations between the subject and the photographer, and I decided I wanted to learn more about them.

Dad was also oblivious to a shoebox filled with letters he'd written Mom, and next to it another of those she'd written back to him. I'd read those too. They were all in order, only one letter she'd written seemed to be missing from one of the stacks tied up with string.

I looked up at the bedroom window and realized Mom was also watching him. She soon came downstairs and walked toward the garage.

"You're not going to find the answer in a book," Mom called out, gathering up the bucket he'd left on the driveway.

"I can help her. It's a medical problem."

"No, it's not."

Then Mom gave him her own answer. She dumped the leftover mixture of soapy water and rags onto the clean car. I stepped back from the window, making it a frame, and I imagined how I would contain what I'd seen. There had been Dad, a still figure under the eaves, and Mom, her arms in motion over the hood of the car, and I thought about the photographs I'd seen in the magazines. For the first time, it was the camera, not the darkroom that I wanted as my third eye.

Dad didn't react immediately to what she'd done, only watched her from afar, like a soldier on patrol, scouting out new territory.

"Evie, please."

"You can't ask me to do this," she responded. "It's not right. I've accepted it all, haven't I?"

"Yes, you have."

"But you want more. It's not right," Mom continued.

"I know." He went over to where she stood, still studying her, her new assurance, but now as though she was an X-ray, examining her for fractures, dark spots. "She's sick, Evelyn. The child is ill, I think I can help her."

Who is sick?

I wanted to cry it out, but I didn't want them to know I was listening in on them, spying.

It was the same war, but with different rules of engagement. Their arguing was quiet now, like paper cuts, almost unnoticeable, and I wished they'd go back to slamming doors.

"You have to give me time."

"She needs me," he said, and it was a plea.

"She can't come here now," Mom said.

She.

It was a short word, hardly a syllable, almost a shush, and I strained to hear more.

"I don't care if you see her. I won't even mind Lucy seeing her, but I don't want her here, in my—" Mom stopped mid-sentence when she saw me near the open window.

Mom and Dad looked at me.

They were both in my crosshairs now, and I could have confronted them. It was in my hands, my call. They were waiting for me to ask them, aching to tell me, but I didn't want to hear it.

"I'm going to Diane's house," I called out to them through the window, but went up to my darkroom instead. I sat on the stool and put my head on the table, closed my eyes.

I fell asleep right away.

❧

I was in the mattress department of Bullocks once again. I hadn't been there in a long time, and the displays had all been changed around, but the beds were still lined up as they always were, like cots in an army barrack. I waited until the salesman was distracted by a younger couple trying out a new Sealy Posturepedic. They sat down on the mattress together and the man fell back first, like a sack, then his wife.

I eyed the beds furthest away, near the television sets in the electronics section.

I was tired, my legs giving way and I lay down on one of those sky-blue mattresses, bare, like a raft on a river.

Get a good night's sleep with Beautyrest, the sign said.

Above, *Let's Make a Deal* played on thirty TVs.

I made my own deal with Monty Hall.

Just ten minutes.

Let me sleep for ten minutes.

Save me.

Then the store melted, gave way to a wide boulevard of trees and statues, benches and flocks of graying pigeons. The ground trembled, and steam rose up from metal grates. A late afternoon light gilded the tops of the buildings. Then rain fell, and lightning cut the sky. I woke up to its electricity and I switched on the lamp.

All the dreams I hadn't remembered suddenly found their way to me, all their parts and pieces, glassy slivers, like wavelengths of light captured in crystals of silver, in the emulsion of film. I wrote them down.

Mai

I said goodbye to Thanh, Cousin Hong and Do at the ticket counter in Charles de Gaulle, and I felt it, a sensation that something was about to change. I didn't want them to accompany me to the gate, and Nguyen and I took one of the glass-enclosed escalators connecting the terminals like moons orbiting around a planet. I felt it again, slowly, as we waited at the gate, and I sat on one of the chairs in the waiting area, linked one to the other. Then it happened once more, when I boarded the Air France jet that would take me to California. It was just a subtle change in pronoun, a small adjustment, a minute linguistic shift. I didn't think of him as *her* American, Linh's American, anymore. He no longer belonged to her. He was mine.

And from that moment, he took on a new name.

My American father.

I couldn't simply think of him as "father," and his first name, Aaron, the name Linh had called out in the night, felt amiss to me as well, but "my American father" was apt. After all, he was merely one of the many others, all the Americans who had fathered children in my country.

Linh would have understood.

It was only fitting, this new alignment of words.

And it seemed right too that I was leaving Paris in *Mai*, French for the month of May. Linh would have appreciated the concurrence; she would have said it was no coincidence.

Outside the window, the plane's wing stretched out into the long, tangerine horizon. I looked down at the watch my American father had given me at the restaurant. The watch had a metal strap and I eyed its roundness. I took it off, saw how the impression it had made on my wrist stayed, then slowly disappeared. Nguyen sat next to me, reading a book about California. I could see he was battling sleep and I envied the way his head dropped with a jerk to the side. I was jealous of his sleep and he roused, shook himself out of his stupor. Linh should have been with me on the plane to Los Angeles; Linh, not Nguyen, but she was gone. Like the indentation of a watch, she'd faded too. Her disappearance was her last gift to me. My American father would never have taken me away from her to Los Angeles, if she hadn't disappeared. He did many things, but he wouldn't have done that to her.

I looked over at Nguyen. He thought he knew me, but he was mistaken. He confused me with one of his myths—Medea or Medusa, Minerva or Mnemosyne. He was a student of their stories and wanted them to come alive in me. I hoped to love him more, but now I only needed him to bring me to California, to stand between me and my American father, like a buffer, a demilitarized zone, so that my American father would know I didn't come cheap, that he'd have to work for me.

"How are you feeling?" Nguyen asked me.

"I don't want to talk."

"Then I'll talk for the both of us," he said, cheerily.

Nguyen then told me about California and Los Angeles. He described the spine of the state, the San Andreas fault-line that cracked a path from the North to the South.

"Is there a Metro?" I asked, suddenly interested.

"No, there are no subways in Los Angeles."

I was sure I wouldn't like a city without a subway, without tunnels, where the earth moved and buildings fell. Where would I hide when I needed the earth to be my blanket? I didn't like the way my American father had called it "L.A." How could I live in a city whose name could be shortened so easily?

When we arrived, Los Angeles was hot, burning like Saigon. My American father met us at the gate in sunglasses, his collar unbuttoned. Beads of sweat rose above his upper lip, a wetness stained the underarms of his short-sleeved shirt. All that time he'd spent in Vietnam and he'd learned nothing. He'd never learned how to bear the heat. I could see he fought it instead of letting it in, instead of surrendering to its allure.

He was alone, a bouquet of wilting flowers in his hands.

"I'm so happy you're here," he said.

"Yes, we're here."

I didn't expect to see his wife and the girl. I knew they wouldn't come, but I wished he'd have brought them. I would have understood him better if I'd seen them, would have seen what kind of a father he was, what sort of a husband he'd been. I would have known it in an instant. I would have noticed the way they talked to each other, the words they used. Their faces would have told me what I needed to know. They would have been my reconnaissance.

In the car, I sat in the front. Nguyen was unhappily exiled to the back seat. I looked out the window. Everything was flat here, the sky too bright; it was a monotony of blue. I tried to find something familiar, anything that would give me comfort, but even the stretch of palms within the airport did not console me.

On our way out of the complex, we passed a round building floating in the air on spider legs, and I thought it was a bad omen. How would I stand this city without tunnels?

And then I saw it. From the highway, I could see glimpses of it carved below. It looked like a river, but it was encased in concrete, fenced in. The sign said it was called the L.A. River, but it wasn't a river at all, just a storm drain. I'd see it on my left, and then it reappeared to the right, like a snake. Entombed as it was, I could see seedlings pushing through the tiny cracks, daring it to be a river once again. I could feel the arteries of water, the tributaries below me and I knew I could endure it here.

On the way to Nguyen's family, my American father stopped at a McDonalds drive-thru. Nguyen ordered a chocolate milkshake. "How about you, Mai?" my American father asked me.

I shook my head.

"I'm not hungry."

Do you think I've never eaten a hamburger?

I wanted to recall what Linh had once said about the word "ketchup," how she'd laughed at its strange origins, but I couldn't remember. Was it derived from the Chinese or born in Malaysia? Why couldn't I remember?

"This is Orange County," he explained, when we got back into the car. "It's not far from Los Angeles."

"But I see no orange trees here," I said.

"They're calling it a 'Little Saigon,'" Nguyen squeaked from the backseat.

"For now, you'll stay with Nguyen's uncle, Pho," my American father explained. "Later, maybe you'll come and be with us."

"Maybe."

I turned around and looked at Nguyen, sulking now in the backseat. He didn't want me to live with my American father. He knew there would be no place for him there, if I moved to the doctor's house.

We arrived at a pink house with a green lawn.

My American father parked but didn't turn off the ignition. He handed Nguyen a piece of paper. On it, he'd written down a list of instructions, telephone numbers and addresses, sleep exercises and herbs. He also gave him a notebook with directions for filling in a sleep-diary. Nguyen smiled, now that he was the doctor's assistant, my American father's newest set of hands. Nguyen opened the trunk and took out our suitcases. He carried them to the house and greeted his uncle at the door.

For the first time, I was alone with my American father. He left his car door open and came around to say goodbye. He'd come back and see me in a few days, when I was settled, he said.

"We'll talk then, get to know each other. You're probably tired," he continued, "jet-lagged, from the plane ride. I want to give you time." It was the most he'd said to me, and his words came out rushed, slamming up against each other as if there were no spaces between them, no punctuation. Then he stroked my cheek and turned around to go back to his driver's side.

Coward.

He hadn't yet asked me about Linh. He hadn't even said her name. As though he was driving a getaway car, he kept the car engine running, ready to flee.

I didn't move.

Don't leave me yet.

Don't leave me again.

Then I saw her.

I wasn't sleeping. I wasn't dreaming. I was completely awake. She wasn't there, but I felt her presence. I felt Linh's face and hands, saw her silken hair. And when I saw her, I knew I missed her, ached for her. She'd come to see me, to watch over the reunion she'd planned and conjured, wished for, and then, given to me—her mother's gift.

He stopped and came back to me, but he could only look down at the ground.

Say it. Say you're sorry.

"I tried to get the two of you out. I pp-promise you I did," he suddenly stuttered, but this time, his tiny stammer gave me hope. "When I realized that Saigon was going to fall, I tried to come back, but it was impossible, too late. I called everyone I knew, all my contacts in the State Department, anyone who could help. No one thought it would happen so fast, that the city would fall so quickly."

I tried to imagine it—Saigon, falling. But I couldn't understand. How did a city fall? How did an entire city tumble, topple like a tree, cut to the ground? How was there no one to catch it when it fell?

"I tried to find your mother...and you. I tried everything I could. Do you believe me?" he pleaded. He continued talking, but I couldn't listen anymore. He was an anarchy of words crossed out, illegible on a page.

Say her name.

He didn't move.

Then Linh's spirit took hold of me.

Help him.

How can I?

I wanted to believe him, but I didn't know whether I could, whether I should. I saw it all clearly. Linh, mad as she was, had filled up all his holes. She'd found the places where no one had touched him. Linh and her words. While he'd been her rescuer, her destroyer.

I reached out to touch him.

"I never regretted you," he said.

Her words came back to me now, beautiful and spare. Regret— it was from the French word, *regretter,* to lament over the dead, and the word was precise in its imagery. Somewhere in Vietnam, we'd all died.

He must have seen her, felt her too because he fell silent, and he draped his arms around me and we both wept. We cried for her.

"Linh," he said.

Lucy

E verything seemed sluggish, the cars, the clouds almost still, the trees streaking green on both sides of the freeway. Summer had slowed the city, stretching out the daylight. Even Dad was driving slowly, as if in a convoy, as though he too wanted to spread open time, loosen it away from the present. It had been months since he'd come back from his trip, and he drove with only one hand resting on the lower part of the wheel, as if he were saving his energy, storing it up for some emergency. Dad didn't say much. I was used to his quiet, when he folded himself up like the *L.A. Times* he read every morning. I watched the road ahead for a while, noted the dotted lines in between the lanes. I'd passed my driver's test, but I wasn't interested in driving anymore, now that I could. Dad never once crossed over the lines, not even a bit, like Mom sometimes did; his driving was always precise. After we passed the airport, I fell asleep, and didn't wake up until we reached our exit.

I woke up to the curl of the off-ramp over the freeway. The sharp turn then opened up to a wide street with rows of stores. Mint-green pagoda-like roofs popped out of the top of mini-malls, fake like Disneyland. I read the names of the stores to myself.

Bao Hien Xe, Ngoc Bridal, Van's Bakery.

Dad pulled into the parking lot of a stripmall. "Aren't we going to a clinic?" I asked. I'd thought Dad was taking me along to one of the clinics he often volunteered at on Saturdays.

"No. We're going to meet them here."

"Meet who?"

"Someone I want you to know. It's better this way," he said as he turned off the ignition and jumped out of the car.

What way?

I followed him to the entrance of the mini-mall. Beyond the red-framed doorway, the mall was noisy, crammed with little shops spilling over into the main hallway. There was a music store blasting Asian pop, a dress shop that sold tea and herbs. And alongside the shops, there were several kiosks. Plastic toys and wind chimes lined one display, while jade figures of Jesus mixed with bonsai trees in another.

Dad seemed to know exactly where he was going, leading me by the elbow, weaving through the crowded mall.

"Here we are." He stopped in front of the New Phuoc Loc Tho Restaurant, where a waiter stood hawking laminated menus to the passersby. "We're meeting them here," Dad said, as the waiter ushered us to a corner table, closest to a large fan. The table number was stenciled on the wall above the Formica table, like an army mess hall. "Here, why don't you look over the menu, see what you want to eat," Dad said, handing it to me.

"I'm not hungry."

"They're late," Dad said, checking his watch, then glanced in the direction of the entrance.

I sat down at a table, but Dad remained standing and spoke to the waiter in Vietnamese. He was anxious, alert to every sign of movement.

Near the front counter were bundles of greenish sugar cane, tied and stacked in a corner. Stringed lights flashed on and off, falling like spider webs over the mirrored walls. A man's voice crooned sleepy ballads in Vietnamese over a speaker that was perched on the wall. It was too hot to eat. I studied the iced fruit drinks on the menu—pennyworth leaves, soda with milk and egg, coconut juice, liquefied jackfruit and soursop.

"I just want something to drink with lots of ice." I was suddenly thirsty.

"They're here," Dad said out loud, then walked over to the doorway to greet a young man and a girl. Dad spoke with the man for a moment, then pointed to my table. I craned my neck, but couldn't see very much. The three walked over to where I was sitting.

The girl looked a little younger than me. For a moment, I thought she was Doan. She had a tiny moon face.

But she wasn't.

"This is Mai," Dad said.

"Mai," I repeated, and her name was a plum in my mouth, sweet and tart.

"And this is Nguyen," Dad introduced the young man.

Mai sat down across from me but didn't say a thing. Nguyen stood stiffly behind Mai.

The girl looked tired.

"It's getting worse," Nguyen said, but he wasn't talking to Dad. He seemed to talking to me. He spoke English softly, with an accent. "I've stayed up and watched her. She's not sleeping at all now, not even a minute. I don't understand how a person doesn't sleep, night after night. It's not possible."

"Let's all sit down," Dad said, trying hard to sound calm. He was usually good at being in charge, telling people what to do, but not today.

"Nothing you've suggested has worked," Nguyen accused Dad.

I looked at Dad and Nguyen. They both drew themselves up and there seemed to be a tug of war between them.

I got up and moved to the empty seat near Mai.

Mai's face was blank. "I don't understand why they fight like that," she said, turning away from Nguyen and Dad. "It doesn't help when they fight." Like Nguyen, she too spoke perfect English, but her English darkened the edges of her mouth, stained them with a strange pitch.

"Maybe I should talk with Mai alone," I announced. I wanted to get her away, separate her from them.

"They think they know what's best for me," Mai spoke out again. "But they know nothing. They think it's their fault I don't sleep. I keep telling them—it doesn't have anything to do with them. They blame themselves, but it's me. I can't sleep. It's only me. I did it to myself."

"We'll go." Dad offered.

"Yes. We'll take a walk," Nguyen said, surrendering.

I reached over to touch Mai's hand. She was very thin. She was so pretty, like Doan. I hadn't thought about Doan for a long time.

She was the daughter of Bao, one of Dad's Vietnamese friends who'd worked for the American embassy. After Saigon fell, he and his family ended up at Camp Pendleton with the first wave of refugees. Doan didn't speak much English at first, but every Sunday afternoon for a year, Dad brought her to the house and we invented our own language. One day, the visits stopped and I never saw Doan again. When I'd asked Dad about it, he'd said her family had moved to Seattle, but I'd always thought it was Mom who had something to do with Doan not coming over anymore.

Mai didn't say a word. I reached over for Mai's hand again.

"Don't." This time, Mai pulled her hand away. "Everyone who touches me stops sleeping. Nguyen—he can't sleep anymore. He watches me and, worries."

"That's not true, Mai. And anyway, it doesn't matter to me. I'm used to not sleeping. I can stay up for hours."

"You can?" Mai looked up at me.

There was so much to tell her.

I nodded. I wanted to tell her about my dreams, the ones that were like rivers, twisting, the others that spilled into strange deltas and streams, caves, swallowing the night.

No, not now. I can't tell you yet.

"So you know how it feels?" Mai asked.

"Yes. And touching has nothing to do with it."

"There are many ways of touching," Mai said and I understood her immediately, as though the thought had been my own. She shook her head and looked toward the entrance to the restaurant. "Your father wanted to tell you, but I think I should do it. I should be the one."

"Tell me what?"

Before Mai could answer, Dad and Nguyen came back to the table and sat down. I wanted to stop Dad from saying it, but too late.

"Mai is your half-sister," he blurted out.

Dad watched me carefully, but I didn't react.

Don't tell me.

I already know.

But how could a sister be a half?

Which half was she?

"Lucy, say something."

"What do you want me to say?"

I was mad, I was angry, but not about Mai—about Doan. Dad had brought her to me years ago, and made me love her, as if I were rehearsing, practicing to love Mai one day.

You can't do that. You can't exchange one person for another, and make a substitution. Dad had brought me here to meet my sister, but I already knew that. She wasn't a stranger to me, this girl with a tiny face, a girl who couldn't sleep. I'd seen her image, spent the night with her, many times before.

I knew all about her.

Mai

In the morning, there wasn't a promise of a cloud in the sky, not even a hint of shelter. The sun pressed against the earth, lighting the air up like a torch. Nguyen borrowed his uncle's car for the day, insisting we leave early so I could buy some new clothes before meeting Lucy. I still had the envelope full of cash my American father had given me when I'd arrived in California, and Nguyen suggested we go to some of the small, elegant shops in Newport Beach. He'd taken me to those kinds of stores before—carpeted and hushed like the stores in Paris, with well-dressed salespeople asking if we'd needed help. He was unhappy when I told him to drive to the KMart, where Pho's daughter, Anh, had taken me the week before, and we argued the entire way there.

"This is not a place for you," Nguyen said when he pulled into the parking lot. As if to dissuade me, he parked the car in a spot furthest from the store. "You should have more, and I will give it to you."

"This is what I want," I said.

I went into the store and chose a shopping cart, and Nguyen followed.

I could see he hated the waxy linoleum and the music piped in over loudspeakers. He didn't understand the landscape of my aloneness, my solace in the geography of rows of air fresheners and cleaning supplies.

It's easier to be alone here.

I liked the dull shelves of Pyrex and action figures, and the racks of blue jeans, their wideness. Nguyen sniffed at the white, polyester blouse and sneakers I picked out, but I forgave him because he wouldn't be going with me on the journey I was about to take. I pulled out the pinkish shoelaces from their eyelets and wrapped them around my wrists. Just like the laces of sisterhood, they too tied together two ends.

I looked around. There was a large family, parents and five children clustered around their cart. Some of the children then scattered down the aisles, yelling out the items they wanted their mother to buy, but the smallest girl remained, pulling out a plastic baby Jesus from inside the lowest shelf. Leftover from Christmas, it had been tucked away, forgotten, in the clearance section. She showed it to her father, and he cradled it in his arms for her, whispered to her to kiss its cheek.

"We're going to be late," Nguyen insisted, tapping on his watch, but I ignored him, pushing the cart through the store, going up and down each aisle. "It's not right to keep them waiting," he persisted, when he caught up to me.

I've waited.

Linh waited.

And I savored each pass of the second hand on the wall clock. I looked up and saw myself in the mirror slanting down from the ceiling. There was no need to hurry. Time was unfolding, revealing itself, making its own appointments.

After I'd been down every aisle, I paid for the blouse and sneakers at the cash register, and then changed in the ladies room.

Back in the car, Nguyen was more anxious than ever, driving fast and changing lanes, cursing the red lights. We were already half an hour late when we arrived at the restaurant. Nguyen and my American father had chosen the restaurant, but I would have picked a different place, something familiar for her sake, for Lucy, for what we were about to tell her, but they were men, and they didn't comprehend the nuances of gesture, of place and time. I knew it would be up to me to find a way to protect her from their complacency.

From the doorway, I saw Lucy, sitting at the table. She wore shorts and a simple white T-shirt, bright in the dim room, and I felt the hole inside me closing itself up with its clarity. We walked over to the table, and I didn't need to embrace her, just seeing her, just the breath of her was enough.

My American father introduced everyone, and then left me alone with Lucy. We spoke for a while, but I barely listened to what she was saying at first. I was studying her, watching the way she drank her lemonade, the form her lips took when she spoke, how she crossed and uncrossed her legs. Everything about her was a mirror. I'd already made up my mind—I'd be the one to tell her who I was. But he returned too soon.

"Mai is your half-sister."

They were only five words, but it was as if the room vanished. It felt like a grenade had taken all the sound, took out the walls and the ceiling, and it seemed a familiar place to me, this vacuum in the midst of an explosion.

No one spoke, not even Nguyen who hated every silence.

I looked at my sister and told her with my eyes. I'm sorry, Lucy, I'm sorry that it was like this.

Then it came to me, suddenly, like a daydream.

"I want to go to a movie," I said.

"What?" Nguyen and my American father asked, almost in unison.

"We want to go, Lucy and I," I corrected, and the word "we" echoed inside of me. It was the first time I remembered saying the word, this plural, this union of me and another.

"Well…all right, if that's what you two want," my American father said, still puzzled by the timing of my request, but there was no confusion in Lucy's eyes. She instantly understand and nodded yes. She saw exactly what I saw—the theater, its rows of seats, the screen lit up.

"Yes, *we* do," Lucy finally spoke.

"I'll get a newspaper," Nguyen said, trying to make himself useful. When he came back to where we were sitting, he flattened out the paper on the table and pored over the movie listings.

"Not too much playing in the middle of the day," Nguyen announced.

I was about to say something, but it was Lucy who explained. "It doesn't matter what we see."

Reluctantly, Nguyen went back to his uncle's house and my American father drove Lucy and me to a run-down movie theater in Garden Grove. Black against white, the letters on the grooved marquis spelled out *Star Wars*.

"I'll come in with you," he said, as he pulled into a parking space.

"You can pick us up later," I said.

"But...."

"We want to be alone," Lucy clarified.

"Then I'll wait for you outside in the parking lot," he said.

"It's a long movie. " Lucy continued.

"I'm not leaving you," he insisted. "I'm not leaving anymore."

We bought tickets for the matinee and went inside. The lobby was dusty and smelled of stale popcorn. The theater was almost empty, and we could have chosen any seat, but we picked two on the last row. We sat through the movie once, then again, knowing it would be late by the time the second show let out. There in the dark, the theater was a womb of craters and moon rocks, opalescent, and we were two planets born and ruined, resurrected in Princess Leia's galaxy.

And our father didn't leave, he waited for us in the parking lot.

Lucy

On the way back home in the car, Dad tried to talk to me, but I didn't want to hear what he had to say, and turned away from him to look out my side window. The scenery outside was exactly the same as when we'd left in the morning, but it wasn't. Everything had shifted, like a change in focal length, perspective. There was hardly any traffic on the freeway, and it seemed wrong to me that we were already headed home fast. It was too easy.

"Lucy, I need to talk to you."

"I don't want to talk."

"Let me explain," he appealed to me.

"Not now."

After a while, he gave up and just drove. When we returned home, Mom was waiting for us on the driveway, a light shawl draped over her shoulders. As hot as the day had been, the night air had brought a chill, but her shawl hung loose, and I could tell by the way the fringes brushed the ground that she'd forgiven him. We were the ones coming back from Orange County, but she'd made her own journey, and absolution was a road she'd often traveled. Even if she hadn't yet forgiven herself—for letting it happen—she'd pardoned him, once again.

Two weeks later, I was alone in the house. Mom and Dad had gone to my parents' lawyer to sign some papers. The doorbell rang and I saw Nguyen through the peephole. He was looking around, standing a few steps back from the door, and his eagerness made him seem shorter than when I'd seen him at the restaurant with Mai.

"I'm sorry, I think I'm early," Nguyen said, when I opened the door. "Your father said I could meet him here."

I looked out into the street to see if Mai was in his car or on the driveway, but she wasn't.

"Come in," I said, as I held the door for him.

I showed him to the living room and we sat together on the sofa.

"Do you want something to drink?" I asked, not knowing what to say, but I didn't mind being alone with him.

"Yes, please," he said politely. "Something cold."

I got up and went into the kitchen to bring two glasses of ginger ale. When I came back to the living room, he was leafing through one of the books on the coffee table. I liked the way his hair fell on his forehead. He dropped the book on the floor, then picked it up.

I'd overheard Mom and Dad talking about Nguyen, how he wanted to marry Mai. Dad had been upset, when he'd told Mom that Mai's grandmother had agreed to an engagement on the condition that Nguyen wait until Mai turned eighteen.

Nguyen took a sip of the ginger ale. He spoke first, but he sounded rehearsed, as if he'd been practicing.

"Mai was standing right under the center of the Eiffel tower," he began, as if he was telling a story. "There were hundreds of people around, but I only saw her, couldn't keep my eyes off of her. It was as if she wanted to lift the tower up all by herself," Nguyen said. "It was so beautiful to see her there, in that place," he said, his eyes lighting up.

I put down my drink and hoped he would tell me more.

"Tell me about Paris," I asked.

He sat back and continued talking. He loved the grayness of

winter over the banks of the Seine, the booksellers. The Ile Saint Louis lodged in its heart, he said. He knew everything about the city, its architecture and wide boulevards. France flowed in his Vietnamese blood.

Nguyen studied Greek mythology at the Sorbonne, and lived with his family on the Avenue Mozart in the sixteenth *arrondissement*, he went on. He was born in Paris and had never been to Vietnam, he explained.

"Not even for a visit?" I asked.

"It doesn't have anything to do with me. All that's done, over with. Everything's ruined. Why would I want to see the bomb craters, the statues of Lenin and Ho Chi Minh," he asked out loud, but he wasn't asking me. "I don't understand her."

He was calling out to Mai, asking her why she sometimes yearned to go back there, to her *que huong*, her homeland, what drew her back to the destruction there, and her own rubble. Or maybe he was asking himself. Despite his protestations something had drawn Nguyen back to it as well, through Mai, and it was as though he were standing on the steps of his own burned-out house, needing to find out what had come before.

"You'll have to visit us," he said, gulping down the soda I'd brought him. "When we get married. I'm going to marry Mai, one day, you know. I'm her fiancé."

"I know."

"Will you come?"

"I don't know."

He was talking as if everything had been settled, a photo already snapped, a moment memorialized.

It was getting dark in the room and I wanted to get up and turn on the lights.

"Do you want some more soda?" I asked, starting to get up.

"No. Sit with me," he said, catching my arm.

He moved closer to me on the sofa. "I'm so tired." He closed his eyes for a moment. "Mai stopped sleeping and all I want to do is sleep. The Greeks called the god of sleep Hypno, and his son, Morpheus the god of dreams," he said. His face was inches from mine.

"They understood human nature more than any civilization. They had a god for each of our weaknesses."

His words were falling like feathers all over me and I wondered whether he was trying to hypnotize me.

"It will be good for Mai to know you, to know her sister," he said as he suddenly took my hands, turned them palms up to examine them. "It's not the eyes that are the windows to the heart, it's the hands. You have very long lines."

"Where?" I looked at the lines that stretched from my wrist to above my thumb, the creases that marked my hand.

"See, here," he said, gently tracing the lines with his finger. He turned my hands over.

I took a breath. Everything about him was a soft smoothness, his face, his hands. Nguyen smelled good, like almonds.

I wanted to be Mai, and for a moment I was her. I was in Paris, the gravel of its paths, soft beneath my feet. I was underground, in the dark, a train of light in my head. I was her, crushed, and broken, bones and shells.

"You're her sister," Nguyen whispered, as if he were praying, as though he were giving me a clue. "But I'm so tired," he said.

And his head found its way to my lap, nestling there.

I could see he loved Mai. He was here for the part of me that was her. Like all the rest of us, he too was collateral damage, another of my father's casualties, his fate sealed the day Dad met Linh.

I stroked his head.

"You will help her sleep. You're the one we've come here for. I know it," he said.

Nguyen hadn't come to see Dad. It was my help he sought.

"But I don't know how to help her."

"You do," he said, with a lover's conviction, and I believed him. I'd fixed things before. In my darkroom, I'd held back the exposure on one side of the picture, to keep the details in the shadows. I'd brought together unrelated elements, cropping delicately as though I was a surgeon performing an operation. I'd made magic, pasting things together that had been apart, creating the unlikely, conjuring the unseen, what the camera never saw, only imagined.

I could do the same for my sister.

Looking down at him I saw he'd also come for a place to rest his head. I was his tent and his head felt warm and heavy, like cream on my lap. I could hear him breathing, unraveling, feel his chest rise and fall, and I watched him sleep.

Mai

I liked Nguyen's uncle, Pho. He was *Viet Kieu,* a Vietnamese who lived outside his homeland. Wounded in the war, he'd work in his vegetable garden in the morning and sit on the sofa in the afternoon, rarely going out. He'd learned much of his English from watching reruns of *I Love Lucy* on television.

One afternoon, he called to his wife, Tuyet.

"Lu-cy is on. Love Lucy."

Tuyet came in from the kitchen and wiped her hands on her apron. Pho asked me to join them.

"Lucy, she's your sister," Tuyet said, pointing to the TV and Pho laughed.

It was an episode Pho had seen before. Lucy was testing Ricky's love by feigning a crisis. When Ricky became impatient with her false alarm, he accused her of "yelling tiger."

"Crying wolf," Tuyet and Pho corrected in unison.

In the next half hour, Ricky was in the kitchen. Smooth-haired, he loosened the bowtie on his shiny tuxedo.

"My duck is cooked," Ricky said.

"What?" Lucy floated into the room on the layers of her wide, black and white skirt.

"My duck is cooked," he repeated.

"You mean, your goose, your goose is cooked," Lucy said and the audience laughed. Linh had been right. Every word was important. Even a duck couldn't be a goose; a tiger couldn't be a wolf.

"Why don't you go out?" I asked Pho.

He laughed again. "I've lived my life. Now, I like to see other people in this box," he said, pointing to the TV.

The telephone rang and Tuyet turned down the volume. She picked up the phone and then passed it to me, wiping her upper lip with a handkerchief. I took the phone from her.

It was Thanh.

"They found Linh." There was no static on the line and her words were clear. "She's dead, Mai. My Linh is dead."

"Where? Where exactly did they find her?" I asked. There was only one thing I wanted to know.

"What difference does it make?" Thanh replied. "She's gone. My Linh, my beautiful Linh is gone," my grandmother cried on the phone.

"She was mine too. I want to know. Tell me."

"It was in the Metro."

I already knew that. It couldn't have been any place else.

"But where precisely?"

"A bench in the *Jasmin* station. But it's all for the best," Thanh said, suddenly calm on the phone.

"What's for the best?"

"They told me Linh died peacefully, in her sleep. We had a small funeral yesterday."

"Are you sure it was there?" I persisted.

"What does it matter?" I could feel Thanh's teeth on the phone, her jaw.

It did matter. It mattered to Linh. It was her last act and I knew she'd chosen the place for its name. Jasmine.

All those times we'd ridden the subway together, she'd been looking for it. It was the word. She'd chosen jasmine for its tiny, white petals, its fragrance, but also for its origins, born of the genus of the ancient olive trees, to accompany her on her last journey.

I blamed myself for not knowing, not recognizing the moment Linh had left her memories behind. It wasn't the only thing she'd left behind.

Why did you do that, Linh? How did you leave me behind?

ૐ

One evening, a few weeks later, my American father came to see me. He said he wanted to take me to his office, the place he called a sleep lab.

"It's a last resort," he said. "I didn't want to bring you there," he continued. "But I've tried everything else."

I didn't want to go, but I looked at Nguyen sitting on the chair in Pho's living room. He refused to sleep while I couldn't and he was worn out, desperate from my sleeplessness. So finally I agreed, not for me, but for Nguyen's sake.

I couldn't love him yet, but I owed him that.

The girl, my sister, the one called Lucy, also came with my American father. I'd been thinking about her ever since we'd met at the restaurant. I wondered what it would have been like to be her, to have had him as a father all this time.

Was he a good father?

I sat in the front seat of the car. Lucy fell asleep in the back.

"I'm so sorry about Linh," my American father said, reaching out to me. "I know you will miss her. We'll both miss her."

"Yes," I said, and I knew that "miss" was a perfect word, because it meant more than a feeling of absence, it also meant a misfire and an avoidance, an escape and a failure, and all these words belonged to Linh.

The freeway was dark, a river of white light on one side, a stream of red brake lights on the other, with the green freeway signs with their arrows emerging and disappearing, like promises from above.

101 North. 101 South.

Go this way.

When we arrived at the lab, Lucy took out a pair of her pajamas from a bag, ones that were too small for her, she said. For a
moment, I was angry at her. Did she think I wanted her scraps, her
hand-me-downs? Then I looked at her and knew there was no pity
in her gesture. Like me, her instinct was to fix things, correct them,
righting old wrongs, and the burden showed on her face. I put the
pajamas on, and she waited in the room nearby until he'd attached
all the wires, set the monitors. I let him do whatever he had to do,
but I knew it would be a waste of time. He was a doctor and he'd
spent his life looking for the right treatment, prescription, the correct
answer. But even I knew there were no answers, only questions; that
it was the questions that were important, not the answers.

He left me alone in the room.

I'm not afraid. I'm afraid.

The wires and the machines didn't bother me, but when he
dimmed the lights, I was happy Lucy came into the room, and crept
right up to the bed. She put her head down next to mine.

I closed my eyes and breathed in her cinnamon gum smell.
Inside her pajamas, worn thin and soft, I was in her skin.

For a moment I was Lucy and I heard the arguments, slamming doors. I heard Evelyn pleading with him.

"What happened over there, what really happened in Vietnam?
Why won't you tell me? I know something happened."

Then I tasted Lucy's tears in my mouth, felt her sob grow in
the back of my throat. I saw Lucy curled up, asleep in the department store, the bare mattress, floating on it like a life raft. I saw the
rows of televisions droning low, like lullabies above her, singing her
to sleep.

I was her and she was me.

I liked her sleepy talk in my ear. She'd come to give me back
my sleep, my dreams, she whispered in my ear. She said she'd gathered
them all, collected them, all my life's blood. It was a transfusion; she'd
give them back to me, now when I needed them.

She spoke quietly, like Linh.

Lucy took out some papers from her pocket and started reading. The papers rustled in her hand and she read all my stories back

to me, returned them, wove them from the beginning to end. She told me things I didn't remember, about myself, about Linh. She knew them all as if she'd lived them herself, as though they were her stories too. I listened to her, heard the tremor in her voice. I closed my eyes and fell back with her through my life, Linh's life, Linh's dreams, but I never fell asleep.

❀

Thanh bears her only child, her daughter, at her maid's house on a moon-less night. The small room is watery, the walls alive. She bears her there and not in the hospital, away from prying nurses, so she can be sure. The infant is born and is quiet, hardly cries out as if she already knows her burden. And though it is dark, Thanh checks her girl child carefully under the light of a lamp, examines her closely to make sure she has no taint, no hint of the melancholy Frenchman Thanh loved when her husband was away on a business trip.

It is a long way from Hoi An where Thanh herself was born, a harbor town where the rivers intersect into the coast. It is a town of many names. There is no harm, no concern in the changing of a name here from Haifo to Haiso to Cotam over the centuries. In Hoi An, the silk shops are full with bolts of cloth; the streets dotted with pepper and porcelain.

Over Thanh's father's house, an eye guards the door. It is a chrysan-themum of sun and stars. Carved carps perch on the rooftop, cranes and storks are carved into the wood for long life. Pomegranates, watermelons and lotus pods accompany children into the world. It is here she plans against the yin, the ghosts of disease and death. It is here she learns to hang up the stalks to repel evil, to banish the snake and the centipede, the scorpion and the toad, but she does not learn her lessons well.

She doesn't mean for it to happen. She doesn't want to care for the Frenchman, but it is seven years since her arranged marriage with the older man. She should be happy, the daughter of a poor merchant from a family of girls, married to a wealthy businessman of Saigon. Not that he isn't kind to her, showers her with gifts, but often he is away on business, he doesn't seem to need her as much as the sad Frenchman she meets at a café.

She sees the Frenchman watching her from his table. It is no leer.

179

His name is André and he is lonely in Indochine, cut off from his family. He cannot live up to the task he is sent to do—to make a profit from his father's coffee plantation. Thanh hears the music in his voice. She hears the two-stringed lute and the sixteen strings of the zither.

It doesn't take her long to forget herself in the melody of the Frenchman's unhappiness and they meet at his plantation in Da Lat. She takes the train, sits and watches the countryside fall away from the rails.

Thanh breathes a sigh of relief.

The features of the child are the fine, delicate features that are all Thanh. The girl has nothing of the Frenchman, his high forehead and thin lips, his coloring, and no one will learn about the affair, she swears to herself.

She swaddles the baby girl. It doesn't take her long to think of a name and calls her Linh, for her gentle spirit. Then she gives the infant to the maid to hold.

The Frenchman never learns he has a daughter.

His family from Lyon comes for him and takes him home to a sanitarium in Paris and Thanh makes her penance. She makes herself useful to her husband, teaches herself numbers and bookkeeping, helps him in his silk business. Thanh cannot bear any more children and she immerses herself in work. With her help, the company thrives. Her husband loves little Linh, buys her trinkets and books, and takes her on his trips to England and France.

The little girl tags along with him everywhere he goes, sits on his lap, and hides under the shiny, wooden desk in his export office in Cho Lon. Thanh is happy he loves Linh, but argues with him about spoiling the child too much. Father and daughter are inseparable and there is little room for Thanh.

Linh grows up beautiful and delicate, but Thanh watches the girl, waiting for the day the gods will exact their punishment for her mistake. And when Linh's first dark times, her slowly encroaching madness appears, Thanh knows it is the mark of the melancholy Frenchman, his only legacy to her.

Thanh cries when Linh meets the American. It is her own history repeated in her daughter. She pleads with her to cut off the affair. The American doctor has a wife, she makes her case to Linh, and there is no hope for a marriage between them. But Linh doesn't want to listen. Thanh begs again, then decides to tell her daughter about the Frenchman, and shares her own terrible secret with her only daughter.

But Linh has no sympathy for her mother's revelation, her infidelity.

Angry at Thanh's interference, Linh doesn't think carefully. She doesn't measure out her words. She divulges Thanh's story to her father. She doesn't realize her words will light a lantern in his head and that Grandfather will become sick, ill with terrible migraines. She doesn't know he will become a gambler and his business will fall apart. She doesn't realize it is her words that tear him apart. It is her words that kill her father, a cacophony of words that stand forever between Linh and Thanh and their forgiveness.

Lucy

It was late September, and grapes burst from the vines tied to the back fence of my grandparents' yard. Mom dropped me off in the early afternoon to help my grandfather make the sweet, amber-colored wine he bottled every autumn. This year, the grapes were already stacked in wooden crates in the garage, and I breathed in their heady smell.

"Come, Lucy," my grandfather motioned to me. "I've been waiting for you."

David wore an oilcloth apron and sat on a low stool, the unwashed grapes to his left and dozens of large, clear bottles on his right. Each year, it was my job to separate the smooth-skinned orbs from their tumbling clusters, dropping the sticky fruit, one by one, into the clean dry bottles. After an hour, my hands were stained purple, gummy with pulp. When the containers were three-quarters full, I handed them over to my grandfather who sifted sugar into the bottles through a large, metal funnel, like sand draining down through the opening of an hourglass. After sealing it, he cleaned off the bottles with cheesecloth and labeled them, carefully marking the date with a waxy red pen. He then lined most of them up along with the older bottles that were aging on shelves in a cool corner of the garage.

Ruth came by and stood by the door to watch us.

"Your grandfather made a bottle for you the day you were born, Lucy," she announced.

"Where is it?" I asked. "I want to see it."

"Not now, Ruth," my grandfather glared at her.

"No, she needs to know everything," my grandmother continued, and she pointed to a shelf behind a makeshift curtain.

I went to the shelf and found the bottle with my name and my birth date on it, and took it out. Behind it, another bottle stood. It had Mai's name, and a date, two years after my own.

I put both bottles back in their place and closed the curtain. "So you knew?"

Ruth nodded.

Ruth and David had guarded Dad's secrets but they too wanted to rid themselves now of old pledges, wanting forgiveness.

"We haven't met her yet," Ruth said, as if in reparation.

We all helped sweep up the picked-over remains of stems and leaves left on the garage floor. Ruth was just about to turn off the lights when Dad appeared, and with him, Mai. She'd told me she called him my "American father," as a way of putting distance between them, but when I saw them both standing by the door, flat against the doorposts, waiting for a signal to come in, I knew she'd been his navigator, the one to bring him back to Ruth and David.

Even so, Mai's face was hard, contained, as if all of her was compressed into a box. I held my breath as Ruth walked over to Mai. I was afraid Ruth would walk past her, but she stopped and touched the ends of Mai's straight, black hair. She touched them gently, like the fringes on my grandfather's prayer shawl.

"You've come just in time to put away the last bottles," Ruth said, gently pulling back Mai's hair, the delicate curve of an ear lobe exposed. Ruth understood she was looking into the eyes of a child of devastation, holocaust.

Afterward, we all went into the living room. Ruth turned on the lamps and made dark tea in delicate glass cups. Dad sat next to his parents and they talked quietly. I sat in the armchair across from them, Mai next to me on the armrest.

"Aaron," I heard my grandfather say, and the name sounded fitting on his lips, but he wasn't talking about Dad. He was repeating the biblical story he'd told me many times before. "Moses couldn't speak for himself," David said. "It was Aaron, his brother, who spoke in his name," David continued. "It's a terrible burden to put on a young man, to speak, to accomplish for those who couldn't. We asked too much of you, Aaron," David said.

"Aaron."

This time it was Mai who spoke. She said it again, and Dad looked up to hear his name reborn on her tongue.

It was dark now outside, and I wanted to stay and listen to them. Every now and then, a word in Yiddish fell softly, like a sigh, a hush into the night.

"I wish I knew what they are saying," I whispered to Mai.

"There are words for which there are no translations," Mai whispered back.

"How do you know?"

"My mother, Linh, told me," Mai said. "Let's go outside and let them talk."

She took my hand and pulled me out to the front door. From there, she guided me around the perimeter of the house, following its angles. There was a half-moon following us. Like two explorers, we walked around the house, step by step, as if we were untying knots, freeing the phantoms.

Lucy

The last couple of months went by quickly, but things remained the same between Dad and me. I'd make sure to be in my darkroom before he'd come home from work. He'd tap softly, like the black crows on our roof, but I'd yell out to him.

"Go away. Leave me alone."

"I want to talk to you."

Don't talk to me.

He'd give up easily, and I'd hear his footsteps down the hall.

I spent a lot more time in the darkroom, but I didn't do much printing. Mostly, I wanted a place where I could reason things out. I'd used it before as a space for trial and error, mistakes and miscalculations turned around by refiguring, and it seemed the right place for me to reinvent solutions.

Mom never mentioned Mai, and I was between my mother and my sister, loving them both, each one a ghost, erased, in the other's presence. Never meeting Mai, not mentioning her name, was my mother's way of keeping the cease-fire between her and Dad, and I gave this ruse my reluctant acceptance. She'd forgiven everyone—my father, even Linh, but not Mai. The child born through no fault of her own was the one person Mom wouldn't forgive somehow, her last link to the anger she couldn't let go of.

My own truce with my father came slowly, unexpectedly, when we'd drive down to Orange County to see Mai. I'd bring my camera along, and the three of us would go out to dinner and a movie.

I'd sit next to Mai and watch her struggle. She fought so hard against being loved by Dad. She talked sparingly, every word doled out, the tiniest of compromises. She paid him back now for all that was unspoken for years.

I wanted to tell her. You're just like him, Mai, just like your father, you are your father's daughter.

One night after a movie, we went to a coffee shop and Dad pulled out Mai's case file, spreading the contents on the table.

"Look at these," he said, showing us the graphs and printouts.

That was the moment I started to forgive him, then, when I watched him try so hard with Mai. He didn't know what to say to her, how to act. He was awkward and shy. I watched her face and took out my camera, shot photographs of her just as she was then, beautiful in her ambiguity—wanting his love, not wanting it.

"You've seen the charts on my other patients. What do you think, Lucy?" I looked at the charts. "Go ahead, Lucy. You can explain it to Mai," he said. And I did. I told her everything I'd learned from him. It wasn't that Mai didn't sleep at all. She did. But when she slept, there was almost no REM sleep.

"That's right, Lucy," Dad said. Then he added that he'd never seen anything like it except after Vietnam—with the POWs.

Mai too was a prisoner who'd never come home.

It was late when we dropped Mai at Pho's and headed back home. On the way, the stars streaked small openings of light into the dark sky and they found a chink in my resolve not to ask him.

"Why Linh, Dad?"

He didn't answer right away and we passed two exit signs before he spoke.

"It was wrong, I know. I'm sorry, Lucy. I never stopped loving your mother. You know that, don't you?"

"Yes," I nodded. "But why her, why Linh?"

"I don't know. It was her sleep, somehow."

"I don't understand."

"It was the night we met. Linh didn't have a ride home from the party at the embassy. I had a car and offered to drive her home, but the moment she got into the car, she fell asleep, and I couldn't wake her. I spent that first night watching her. I'd been in Vietnam for seven months. I'd seen everything, but looking at her, it was the first time I cried. She was so alone in her sleep. So alone."

I thought of Ruth and David, of the malevolence of their good fortune, how surviving had cursed them with the absence of the people they'd loved, and how they'd passed that familiarity—the topography of loneliness—down to my father.

※

Mom was quiet when we arrived.

"I can't help her," he confessed, throwing his briefcase on the kitchen table. "I can't." He was talking about Mai, but his words reverberated with a different capitulation. My mother didn't respond, but I could see that something in his simple admission stirred her, and with it a baton, handed over.

Nothing had worked—not all the testing and monitoring, the herbs and medications; not even the hormones, he said. The relaxation exercises had been useless. He'd consulted with colleagues and psychologists from all over the country, but Mai looked thinner, frailer each day. There was nothing more he could do.

I felt sorry for him. He'd helped other people to sleep, even cured some, but he couldn't help Mai.

The next morning, Dad packed for a week-long conference in Chicago.

"I don't want to go, especially now," he said at the front door, and the words seemed worn to him, like a tape recording replayed once again.

"We'll be all right without you," Mom said.

"Are you sure?" he asked.

"I'm sure," she said, and my mother stood tall with some new resolve. It was a firmness that resounded like a hoof against a paddock door.

⅍

A couple of days later, I was in the darkroom looking at some finished prints. The door was open, and all of a sudden a streak of crimson lit up the entryway. It was Mom in her favorite silk dress, Chinese red, clinging to her thighs, just above her knees.

"Are you going somewhere?" I asked, following her to the bathroom. I sat on the edge of the tub and watched her as she put on her makeup. She leaned in close to the mirror over the sink.

"Will you wear the red shoes too?" I asked, as she put on her mascara with a brush, darkening her light lashes.

The red shoes were dyed to match the red dress, but she only wore them on special occasions.

"I don't know," she said, and she blotted her lips with tissue paper, but she looked as if she'd already decided, as though she knew precisely.

"Get dressed too, Lucy," Evelyn said, putting her makeup away in a little zippered case. "You know, I hated that her name, Linh, was so similar to mine. Evelyn, Linh. Strange, isn't it? Somehow that seemed important then, but it doesn't now," she said, stowing the case behind the bathroom mirror. "It all doesn't matter in the end."

"Where are we going?"

She put one finger to her lips as if to say someone was sleeping. "We're going to get her."

"Who?"

"We're going to bring Mai home."

In the car, I started giving Mom directions to Pho's house, but she knew exactly where to go. Mai was alone when we arrived. She didn't look surprised to see my mother, as though she'd been expecting her. She was alone by the windowsill, dressed in her best clothes, her hair combed neatly behind her ears.

On the way home, we stopped for an hour at Manhattan Beach. By the time we reached the valley, it was sunset, and the light

190

was falling away quickly from the sky. The house was dark and Mom turned on all the lights. I took Mai upstairs to show her my darkroom and the photographs I'd printed of her.

Over the past few weeks, I'd noticed my work had changed. I'd spent a lot of time in the library, curious about beginnings, the early Daguerreotypes and the Calotypes, the photos of glass and tin. I discovered the work of early photo pioneers who'd worked with long exposures, I'd pored over their chronicles of lost worlds, the photographic records, the ache of their vistas. I was interested less in revising the image with wild alterations, and had found a balance between the straight print and the fabrications I'd created before. I realized I wanted to achieve neither fact nor fiction and like twilight, I wanted to straddle their divide. It wasn't that I didn't appreciate my old television stills anymore, but the television was no longer a window—it felt more like a blind, and more and more I took my camera out to the streets, snapping portraits of people, finding beauty in the slivers of their lives.

We ate at the dining room table, but it wasn't really dinner, it was more like breakfast. Mom made coffee, squeezing fresh orange juice, eggs and toast, pancakes, and put out the Cheerios box on the table, as if it was morning.

"It's time for you to go to sleep," Mom said, after we'd all cleared and washed the dishes. I thought she was talking to me, but it was Mai she was addressing.

Mai nodded and Mom took her hand, led her up the stairs to the guestroom. Before we'd left to get Mai, Mom had cleaned it, putting fresh linens on the bed. Mai undressed, and put on the same pajamas I'd given her at Dad's office.

"You can go to bed, Lucy," Mom said as I stayed by the door for a few minutes and watched my mother opening up the windows in the room.

It's not going to work.

New linen and open windows wouldn't help Mai sleep. Dad had attempted everything. I'd tried too, the night I'd read to her, but even then she hadn't fallen asleep.

I looked at Mom as she walked around the room. She seemed

so sure-footed, as if she'd grown an extra set of legs. Then I remembered. When I hadn't been able to sleep, it was Mom who'd taken me to the department store and the nail salon. She'd been the one who'd known all the places where sleep hid.

I left them alone, and went to my room across the hall.

I was in bed, listening for sounds from Mai's room, but there was only silence. For a moment I was jealous, thinking of the two of them together without me. I'd already shared my father. I didn't want to share her too. But then I remembered the weeks Mom and I had been alone together, when Dad was looking for Mai.

It was Mai who had given me my mother.

I dreamed I was walking through our house, looking for something I'd lost, when I saw a door I'd never noticed before. It was unlocked and I turned the handle. The door opened to reveal a wing I'd never seen and I was sad I hadn't seen this part of the house. It was enormous, much bigger than the house itself, one door leading to another, like steps on a path, the rooms were decorated with polished woods and beautiful rugs, carefully threaded.

I found a bedroom and the room sank softly around me, and it didn't matter that I hadn't known about it, because everything was here, had always been here.

I woke up with something fluttering, like hands trembling in my head. I walked over to peek into Mai's room. A small nightlight lit the room and I could see that the bed was empty, but the room had my mother's fragrance.

They'd vanished.

I looked again and realized that my mother and Mai were under the bed. Fast asleep, they were curled up on the floor like two ribbons on a package.

I closed my eyes and I could still see Mom, but she was somewhere else. It was another time and she was in a strange room. The walls were bright white, and stark, partition curtains hung limp from ceiling rails. It was a hospital room and she was swallowed, entombed up to her neck by a mountain of metal, a cylindrical tank—her iron lung. It was an ugly thing with little portholes, like a doomed ship. I heard it clanging, echoing; the bellows pushing air in and out; there was her breath against the hard metal. I saw her there, her hands, useless, withered, beside her. She turned her head sideways, and she had the look of a horse that had taken a fall. Over the door, a wall clock ticked, dragging the minutes with it, and I understood everything—why she'd always been in a hurry, why she treasured her hands.

I opened my eyes and Mom was looking at me. I slipped down to the floor and made my way to her.

"She's asleep," Mom said.

"How did you do it?" I whispered to her.

Mom reached out and pulled me toward her. She had a strong grip.

"Come to me, Lucy, and I'll tell you."

"How did you spend an entire year in that iron lung?"

"It saved me. It let me sleep. That's when most polio patients died, you know, when they fell asleep outside the lung. Inside, I wasn't afraid. I was safe. I knew it would keep breathing for me."

I saw my mother there again, the river of electrical cords coursing from the iron lung. The girl who'd lived in her black chamber could only look at her own image, framed in the reflection of the angled mirror rigged above her head. But she knew how to draw things in. Like a radio receiver, like gravity, she'd pulled the world in toward her, collected it. By sheer will, she'd become its magnet, brought it back in with her, into her darkness.

In the worst moments of her young life, Mom had forgiven the iron lung that had made her a prisoner. She'd found a way to harness its power over her, gather in the weakest of signals, the tiniest fragments, every torn shred of a dream.

Mai

I knew Evelyn would come to me eventually. I knew it because I understood her better than she understood herself. I knew her like I knew Linh, every small thing about her. Until now, she'd made sure not to see me, but she hadn't stayed away because she couldn't face me—Aaron's other child. She wasn't afraid in that way. And now that she was coming, it wasn't out of curiosity or kindness, but because she had to, because we were all sewn together with one thread—she, Linh, Lucy, and me. She understood we were one.

I'd known she wouldn't come right away. It wouldn't be like her to do that. She needed time to figure things out and I would have done the same if I were her. I wouldn't have come in haste. I would have thought it through too, planned it, made sure things fit properly, if I were her, his wife. But I knew she'd come when the time was right, because she had to. And I knew she'd come to see me without Aaron between us, in the way. It was our way, a woman's way.

I recognized her immediately, from the window of Pho's house.

I'd come to like standing by windows since the last time I saw Linh, when she stared out the window of Hong's apartment. I liked the idea of windows, their openings and closings, sliding up and down, inward and outward, draped and bare, their way of seeing and not being seen.

I had no doubt it was her when I saw her pulling up to the curb. All afternoon, I'd been waiting by the window, because I didn't want to miss her first steps toward me, her capitulation.

"You're just as I imagined," I said.

"So are you," she answered.

She wore red. I recognized that the color was for me, a flaming red, for we were going to wage war and her dress was her battle flag. She told me her name was Evelyn. I didn't tell her I'd already known her name, that I'd bit my lip practicing the "v" over and over again, ever since I'd first heard her name in Linh's dreams.

When I climbed into the backseat of her car, I noticed her car was different from Aaron's. It didn't have a dark interior, like his. Hers was all cream, like curdled milk. Linh would have chosen *crème* too, I thought, vanilla.

In that they were alike.

Evelyn didn't ask me any questions on the drive to her house, didn't ask me about the new school I was attending, or inquire about Nguyen, or why he'd returned to Paris. I was grateful for her silence, but I would have told her if she'd asked. I would have told her I liked the school in Westminster, but I missed Nguyen, that I would come to see my sister Lucy again in the years ahead, but for now I wanted to go back to my family in France. I needed to return to Linh's Paris.

First, I had work to do, a score to settle, Linh's score. I sat next to Lucy in the backseat, the two of us bunched up against each other in the middle. I wondered whether it disturbed Evelyn to see us that way, like two fruits pressed up together in a bowl, two fruits from the same seed, grown on different trees.

She asked us if we wanted to stop somewhere for a while on the way home. I almost spoke up, but decided it would be better to let her choose, test her. I wondered whether she'd trip up, make a mistake, but I could see she was smart, wily in her tactics, her war strategies. She'd been smarter than Linh. She'd been far away, but she'd reeled him back to her, made him come to her. Linh had lost her battle with Evelyn, but I wouldn't.

I wouldn't make Linh's mistakes.

I looked at Evelyn, at the back of her head, its soft nape, and there was clemency in the way she drove and for a moment, I grew weary of my mission, tired of combat.

She drove us to the beach. We took off our shoes and socks and walked to the water, waded in the water. The sun was still high over the horizon and Evelyn bought us chocolate ice cream cones. They melted, tacky on our fingers and we sat and watched the tide, the water go in and out. It was the place all the waterways emptied into, and then I realized she was even more sly than I thought. Across the Pacific lay thousands of miles of water and beyond that, the China Sea and the bodies of the dragons. She'd taken me to the beach to show me where I'd come from, where I belonged.

Like a compass, she was aiming me toward Vietnam.

We got back into her car and drove northward to my American father's house. After about an hour on the freeway, a round building rose on the left…Then the road climbed upward, and at the top of the mountain range, she exited the freeway. From the summit, I could see the lights of the valley below, the rows of cypress trees. Mulholland Drive, said the blue sign, and the road zigzagged with hairpin turns. She drove fast, and I thought of the Black Lady Mountain once again, wondering whether Evelyn had chosen this road to fling us all down the precipice.

Finally, she took a canyon road down to the other side. It was almost dark when we arrived, but I could tell the house stood on the footprints of a mountain. When we arrived at the house, I hesitated by the doorstep. Lucy and Evelyn went ahead and let me take my time. Finally I entered. Alone inside, I went from room to room. It was the first time I'd seen Aaron's house, and I wanted to search out its core, its essence, find where its corners met and connected. It was his house, but it was a woman's home, with rooms like rivers, winding one into the other. Only his room, his study, had a maleness to it, a certainty of land.

Lucy called out my name.

"Mai."

I didn't answer. I wanted her to call my name out again, hear how my name sounded, echoed in this house.

"Mai! Come upstairs!"

I went up to Lucy and she gave me the photographs she'd made. I looked at them and there was balance between the light and the person it illuminated, the photographs liquid in my hands. Except for my visa papers, they were the first photographs I'd seen of myself, and I saw something altered in my face, something I could never see in a mirror.

I saw Lucy.

I didn't tell her, but I would, at another time, later when we were grown. I would tell her that Linh would have given it her blessing—this union, this love between Lucy and her camera. Linh would have thought it natural, because the two were joined in origin—Lucy, a name born of the Latin word "light," and the instrument that captured it.

Later, I came down to watch. Evelyn was in the kitchen. I wanted to understand the way her hands moved over pots while she was cooking. I didn't dare let her out of my sight for too long, give her a chance to surprise me.

But she wasn't cooking. She was taking out bowls and platters covered with aluminum foil out of the refrigerator. Then she seemed to change her mind and put everything back in the refrigerator.

"I think I'll make breakfast," she announced, taking out a box of pancake mix from a cupboard.

"We'll have pancakes and fruit, eggs and toast," she said, taking out the coffee, as if it were morning. She took out three different kinds of syrups from the pantry, four toppings. Lucy didn't say a word, but I was puzzled.

Maybe you're crazy too, Evelyn, crazy like Linh.

Evelyn made a stack of pancakes on a sizzling griddle, then made more, and brought them steaming hot out to the dining room for us.

By the time we'd cleared the plates, Evelyn said it was late, that it was time for bed, and Lucy and I went up the stairs. Evelyn offered me her hand. I let her take me to the bedroom she'd prepared for me, let her help me put on Lucy's pajamas, tuck me into bed.

I let her think she had won me over with pancakes.

But it wasn't right of her to sit on my bed, stroking my hair with her hand. She had little hands, even smaller than mine and they smelled like Linh's.

"Your mother loves you," she said as she turned off the light on the night table. "Linh loves you."

"Linh is gone." What right did she have to talk about Linh, even say her name?

"She loves you," she repeated. I was going to push her away, drive her off the bed, but I was curious.

"What do you know about Linh?" I demanded.

"I dream about her all the time."

"You?" I cried out. "Not you."

My head felt heavy, a weight on my body.

I'm tired, so tired.

I'd lived with my crimes, taking Linh's dreams, stealing them from her, then sending them away to find Lucy. I knew it was my fault Linh had disappeared, died. I knew it was my doing she'd never come back to me, but this was worse. I didn't know I'd done this too, given away Linh's dreams to Evelyn too, to the enemy.

"No, I've been dreaming about her for years."

"What are you saying?"

"Ever since the night you were born, Mai."

"The night I was born?"

"I always knew about Linh."

It hadn't been me.

I didn't do it.

Linh's dreams had been signals, code from a sinking ship.

Maybe it was Linh's way.

It was how the war was won, and lost, Thanh had told me once, how all wars are won and lost. The conquerors had slept with the enemy, creeping into their sleep, their dreams. It's what the North Vietnamese did when they burrowed under South Vietnam, when they tunneled for miles underneath the American hospitals, their army bases and airports. They slept beneath the Americans, took over their dreams, bored and hollowed into their souls.

Evelyn pulled down all the sheets and blankets to the floor.

Forgiven, the bedding fell to the ground in hills of soft down.

"Come," she pulled me gently to the floor, and gathered me close to her. We flattened ourselves under the bed. "We will both sleep tonight," she said. "And you'll see your mother again. You'll remember everything she told you."

I looked at Evelyn and understood. In my journey to reclaim my father, it was my mother I'd found.

"Mother," I said once, then again.

The word stayed on my lips, soaking them like a balm. The pledge I'd made to my mother was null and void. She no longer wanted me to keep it.

⁊⋲

Aaron wants Linh to deliver the baby at his hospital, at the maternity ward of the Third Field, with his own nurses, the specialists nearby, but Linh refuses. She wants to have the child at home and tells him not to come for the birth. She has determined the chi, the breath of life; she has examined his hospital with a compass and a pendulum, she has taken into account the telephone poles and the crossroads to see where the chi flows, where the yin and the yang, the female and the male lead. His hospital is no place to bear the child.

But when Linh's labor pains come minutes apart, her breath is shallow. Thanh worries and sends a messenger to get him.

Aaron comes back to her—to bring the child into the world, to deliver her with his own hands. Linh is pale when he arrives, but she is glad it is nighttime, that the child would be born to the night. The baby is in breach and Linh cries out when he reaches inside her and turns the child around with his hand. All she sees are the colors of her bedroom, the curtains awash with an orange sunset. But later that night, the city is blacked out and there are no lights anywhere. Even the stars seemed ashen against the sky, obliterated.

After the girl is born, Linh has the strangest dream. It isn't her own, but an infant's dream, a dream of the womb and water, hands, closed lids, and blood, blackness and mountains, as if she is dreaming the dream of her newborn daughter.

She names her Mai, for the color of the cherry blossoms outside.

Linh's sleep is fitful, but each time, she dreams the same dream, and tries to understand it. Thanh closes the door to the bedroom because Linh talks in her sleep, like she always has since she was a child. She fills up the night with words.

And then Linh knows.

Her dream is nothing more than another language for her to decipher. All the languages she's learned and studied, compared and mastered, all the words, the grammar and structures, in English and French, Vietnamese and Chinese, have paled, failed her. The words are barren and there are no words for what she feels for the child, no language, written or unwritten, spoken or silent. Yet, there is a language unexplored and unknown to her, a new tongue.

It is the language of dreams.

She gathers them up, then sends them on a river's journey, but they do not float away until she invokes the mountain. Only the mountain moves the river. Only the force of its descent sends the waters to their promises.

ॐ

Linh has no milk and Aaron bottle-feeds the child himself. He holds Mai in his arms day and night. After three months, he is scheduled to fly out from Tan Son Nhut Airport. He promises to remain with her, with Mai, that he will leave his wife and child, but she knows he won't.

So she tells him to leave. At least that. At least it will be her words that will send him away. It will be her words and her determination.

"Go now. You have no future here," and he leaves her, returning over the years.

Nine years later she tells him again, for the last time. "Go."

The child barely knows her father, but she will, one day, Linh is sure.

They have gone now, the Americans have left. There is already a monument erected to them near the airport. One day it will be overgrown with weeds.

She knows that everything is balance. Where there is a rock hill, an earthy site must be taken. Where there is confinement, an open place must be chosen. Where there is prominence, flatness must be balanced, where strength comes, the weak must be taken, and where there are many hills, there can be water, only water.

This night, she falls asleep. And when she sleeps, she is Linh, but she is also Mai. She is Lucy and Evelyn. Tonight she sleeps the sleep of the dead, the sleep of the living. She sleeps a thousand hours and dreams a thousand dreams. The past and future dissolve, and it is a night of dreams, each one falling onto the other like layers of feathers, falling lightly into the cup of her hand.

Glossary

Ao dai—tunic worn by Vietnamese women

Banh Chung—Vietnamese New Year cake

Bui doi—(lit. "gypsy life"), derogatory term used for children of Vietnamese women and American soldiers.

Celadon—a gray-green pottery glaze, usually pale in color, of Chinese origin.

Cay-*Neu* offering—New Year's tree; a high bamboo pole decorated with red paper to ward off evil spirits.

Cong-San—Communist

Cyclo—passenger vehicle which is propelled by a driver who pedals it like a bicycle.

Donut dollies–women who volunteered to go to Vietnam to help boost morale among the troops. Since one of their jobs was to hand out doughnuts to the soldiers, this slang term became attributed to them.

KIA—killed in action

Lycée—French high school

MACV—Military Assistance Command Vietnam

Non—hat

Nui Ba Den—a 3,000-foot mountain in the Tay Ninh province of Vietnam. It is honeycombed with tunnels and caves, and is also known as "Black Virgin Mountain" or "Black Lady Mountain."

Nuoc mam—Vietnamese fish sauce

Obi—Japanese belt or sash worn around the waist

Pilier sud—south leg of the Eiffel Tower

Quoc ngu—native language

Sampan—an Asian skiff, usually propelled by two oars, often having a sail and a small cabin.

USO—United Service Organization. Provides morale and recreational services to American soldiers.

VC—Viet Cong

Acknowledgments

No book is born without the gentle midwifery of many. Thanks to my devoted agent and friend, Robbie Anna Hare, and to Matthew Miller of *The* Toby Press. To Aloma Halter, my editor, for her insights and thoughtful collaboration. To my generous readers, sisters and brothers in writing—Jacquelyn Powers, Carolyn Howard Johnson, JayCe Crawford, Louise Wheatley, Bob Stone, and John Bernstein. To my friend, Kimsam Vu, and to Robert Harrison, former U.S. Army nurse at the Third Field Hospital of Saigon, who shared their special experiences with me. To my extended family—Yael, Levi, and Ron Galperin; Zachary Shapiro; Dena Marchiony; and the Anducic, Krygier, and Gentile families, who have given me their love and support. To those who have passed away, never forgotten—Rachel and David Halperin, Chinka and Meyer Hornstein, and Ben Krygier. To my children—Oren and Talia, lights of my life, who gave me the courage to write. And to my husband—David, who gave me his hand, and taught me the word "yes."

About the Author

photo: Bonnie Schiffman

Leora Krygier

L eora Krygier was born in Israel and came to America as a child. She lived in France for two years after graduating from law school at The Hebrew University of Jerusalem. A lawyer and a writer for the *Los Angeles Daily Journal*, she has also been profiled in the *Los Angeles Times* for her innovative use of essay writing in her work as a Referee with the Juvenile Division of the Los Angeles Superior Court.

Her debut novel, *First the Raven*, was published in 2002 and she has been a finalist in the Ernest Hemingway Competition, the James Fellowship and the Faulkner Writing Competition. *When She Sleeps* is her second novel. Leora Krygier lives in Los Angeles with her husband and two children.

The fonts used in this book are from the Garamond family

The Toby Press publishes fine writing,
available at bookstores everywhere. For more information,
please contact *The* Toby Press at www.tobypress.com